The
Lake
Still Sobs

ALSO BY MARIE HAVARD

Novels:

Les Larmes du Lac (2015)

Les Voyageurs Parfaits (2010)

Compilation of short stories:

Itinéraires Inattendus (2020)

www.mariehavard.com

ISBN n°979-10-96659-15-9
Cover photo: Editing @Marie Havard
Printed in Poland, US and other countries by Amazon KDP
Published by: Marie Havard France
Independent author

MARIE HAVARD

The
Lake
Still Sobs

The Secret of Lochan Wynd

Translated by

Jacquie Bridonneau

To Luc, Kurt, and Alexander, who I met in St Andrews

*To the memory of my ancestors, Louisette, my grandmother, and
my cousin Alice*

To the memory of Gaétan, Camille and Ange, never forgotten

"When you travel, you experience, in a very practical way, the act of rebirth. [...]

So you are like a child just out of the womb. You begin to be more accessible to others because they may be able to help you in difficult situations. [...]

At the same time, since all things are new, you see only the beauty in them, and you feel happy to be alive."

(Paulho Coelho, The Pilgrimage)

— PREFACE —

This novel is a mixture of true historical facts, real places and imaginary characters.

When I was twenty, I went to St Andrews, Scotland, as a student in the Erasmus program. I fell in love with the city, and today it still seems to me to be a perfect happy place. The year I spent there was the best in my entire life: becoming mature far from everyone I'd known, meeting wonderful people, life as a student and part-time jobs. With this book, I wanted to put the town in the limelight, with its historical richness and untamed beauty.

When you talk about Scotland, its supernatural world cannot be ignored, with its myriad of legends! In St Andrews they are an intrinsic part of its history. I wanted to tell you the story of those who suffered, express History with a capital H (the martyrs, the plague, the witches and so on) as well as telling you ordinary stories (whalers, Elizabeth and Anne's lives, etc.).

I also wanted to include a deeper subject, that of perinatal bereavement. When I was halfway through writing this novel, a dramatic event took place: my son died during childbirth. Finishing this work and then publishing it became a goal for me, something that would help me heal and recover. It was both an outlet and a way to give an existence to stillborn babies. I'll tell you more at the end of the book.

In the meantime, here's Anne's story. Heartbroken, she leaves France to move in Scotland, this country of legends, in a strange house overlooking a lake. Soon, the whispering house and the odd people she meets lead her on an unexpected quest, one that transcends the borders of real life...

— CHAPTER ONE —

I arrived in St Andrews during a stormy afternoon, after having spent the whole night at the airport. An old man smoking a pipe on the front porch of his gray stone house helped me find my way.

"You keep going next to the golf course, then you take the little path running off it, right to Lochan Wynd."

"Thank you!"

He was the kind of person I had been expecting when I thought of Scotland. After walking around the huge golf course, dragging my suitcases behind me, despite how tired I was, I finally arrived. I was still holding the small map I'd drawn to get here with the address on it. I checked it one last time, just to be sure, then I rang the bell at Number 7.

There was moss on the cobblestones in the road, right up to the front steps. The air was humid, it had rained. I realized that one of my bags was in a puddle of water and moved it, angry at myself. I rang the bell again. They should have been expecting me.

Suddenly the door opened, with a long groan. No one was there, so I dragged my luggage up the steps myself.

"Hello. I'm Anne..."

A young man waved at me before disappearing quickly into the next room, visibly having a phone conversation. While I hadn't been expecting a huge welcome, I must admit I was a bit disappointed. I therefore toured the house I would be living in, alone. There was a bathroom, kitchen, living room and a patio on the ground floor. Two half cups of coffee sat on the kitchen table. A nice bow window overlooked the neighboring houses and the narrow road I had taken. I went upstairs where there was another bathroom and three more rooms. Mine was easy to find, it was the only empty one. Green carpeting all over on the upstairs floor. British people seemed to love that color!

My room was ready, just for me: the heating system was on even though it was a mild September, the bed had been made, there were hangers in the wardrobe, the chair extended its armrests as if calling out to me. It smelled good, a mixture of orange and cinnamon, probably straight out of some home fragrance. There were tourist guides on the desk. "You will fall in love with St Andrews timeless atmosphere." I couldn't say I hadn't been warned.

I walked up to the window that opened on the top. Scottish style, without any shutters, but it did have old-fashioned heavy flowered curtains. It overlooked the woods and a small lake with birds. It was calm and peaceful. Perfect for my recovery.

I'd finally arrived, I could relax and appreciate the city, but

14

somehow still felt uneasy. It wasn't just because of the trip, though. Exactly eight months ago, I had lost taste for life, overwhelmed with a permanent loss that nothing could fill. I needed an interlude in this poorly written book that my life had become. I'd left as a punishment and hopefully a new beginning. My *penitence*, my *redemption*. But it was so terribly quiet in this house. Guillaume wasn't there either to hold me in his arms. My heart was with him, and now both were far from me, both were in France.

I started unpacking my stuff. I hung pictures of my friends and family up on the white walls. All of a sudden, I was homesick, looking at these faces frozen in time, knowing that they were so far away. On the back of the door in my wardrobe, I put the photos I loved most dearly: first the one with my parents, raising a toast, smiling. This picture had been taken on Christmas Eve, before it happened. Everyone was still joyful. Next to it, I hung up another one: my laugh was genuine, my eyes were shining, and Guillaume, also elated, was by my side in a suit. When we got engaged, this was one of the best days in my life. I hesitated before taking out the last one but I couldn't help myself. I picked it up and slowly turned it over. Lara, my daughter. I immediately broke down, unable to hold back my tears. So tiny, so fragile... I hung the picture up, gently caressing my baby's profile, then closed the wardrobe door. It still was painful, going far away hadn't changed anything.

I had suddenly lost Lara at the end of six months of pregnancy. Ever since she had left me, it was like I had died with

15

her. It wasn't fair! Everything had started out so well: getting engaged to the man of my dreams, moving to our own place. It was almost as if my wings had been cut off. Or as if I had failed in building our family. It was all my fault; I hadn't been able to keep the baby. I was incapable of giving birth...

At first, I didn't believe it. That couldn't possibly happen, they'd be back and say it was a sick joke. Then, I got mad at myself, furious and sad, I was devastated. I lost my appetite, I couldn't sleep, couldn't stand anyone or anything. My parents had tried to help me, but they were awkward about it and only made things worse. I'd even pulled away from my fiancé. I couldn't understand that Guillaume was playing down what had happened to us, that he didn't tell me about how much he suffered, that he wanted to forget Lara so quickly, turning the page to feel better.

When I saw a pregnant lady or a baby stroller in the street, I cried. Every time someone asked how I was, I felt as if I wanted to be six feet under and wouldn't have to answer. Instead of giving life, I'd created discord and misery. My friends didn't dare show up, fearful that they wouldn't find the right words. My parents kept their distance because I had been awful to them, and Guillaume, the only person I tolerated, took refuge in his work, returning only late in the evening.

I felt like a stranger wherever I went. I resented everyone. Furthermore, I couldn't stand being at home anymore, in this house filled with dreams. Each room confronted me with images of the future I'd imagined: Lara babbling softly in her bedroom, toys strewn all over in the living room, the sweet fragrance of her baby cream wafting through the bathroom. Everything I looked at was heartache after heartache. Then, I found photos of myself when I was pregnant. I had put away all the baby clothes I'd bought, taken down the height chart Guillaume and I had chosen together, dreaming of how big our daughter would be getting. Everything had been taken away from me: my baby, these objects, our future... I was empty.

In this state of despair, I'd decided to go abroad, alone, just to really *be* a foreigner and be far from everything, live in peace, make amends. Going far away to find myself again. But these memories were still fresh in my mind, making it even harder for me to bear the loss of Lara.

Thinking of all this had exhausted me, but I resisted: after all, it was just five in the afternoon. I set off to explore the town to improve my mood. St Andrews was a nice little city and appeared to be a pleasant place to live. It was packed, students everywhere. Each window in the stone-built houses had flowers in front of it. One shop in Market Street made me curious: its windows were already filled with Christmas decorations. The shopkeeper seemed to be a nice old lady, with her long white hair attached in an elegant chignon, bright blue eyes and rosy, pink cheeks. I glanced at a shelf full of figurines.

"They're nice, aren't they? In Scotland we still believe in legends."

She smiled at me warmly. I left after having bought two resin fairy figurines, typical of Scottish folklore. The lady told me they'd help me sleep soundly.

I then took The Scores street which led me to the sea, where I got a breath of invigorating wind. Everything was so gorgeous, I couldn't believe my eyes: the grass, the cobblestone roads, the majestic buildings. The sun was shining, each blade of grass was sparkling. In the South of France, the landscape was so dry compared to here. I was unusually uplifted, perhaps because I was all alone in a foreign country.

I walked to the beach and sat down to admire the sea, its tide going out slowly, leaving behind a huge amount of wet and smooth sand. Seagulls were wading, making triangular marks, which were then washed away. I looked up at the town, perched on a rocky outcrop. A couple holding hands walked in front of me, like a photo taken in the setting sun.

A few drops of rain began to fall, and I noticed some dark clouds racing across the sky from the sea. I started off, but the rain beat me back and the heavens opened. I was utterly soaked in just a few seconds. I began running; my clothes were stuck to my skin, and it was really uncomfortable. I tried to pick up the pace. The house showed up at the end of the road, lit up like Eden. I finally reached the door. It was open and I rushed to take shelter from the driving rain.

Three men were looking at me from the living room, smiling.

"Here's our little Frenchie! Looks like you had a close run with our typical weather here."

That was Mathieu, the French teacher I'd been in touch with before the trip. I took my coat and shoes off as they were leaving footprints in the hall and joined them. They all got up.

"Hi, I'm Alex."

He was tall and thin, with thick glasses and curly black hair. The only thing missing was a pair of bell-bottoms and he would have fitted right into the sixties.

"I'm from Birmingham."

"And I'm William."

William was blond with blue eyes, wearing a yellow and blue striped t-shirt and flip-flops. He had an American accent.

"Where are you from?"

"L.A."

L.A.: Los Angeles, California, this distant and unreal megalopolis. Mathieu handed me a cup of tea.

"Here, this will warm you up."

"Thanks, I wasn't expecting a cloudburst like that! The sky was so nice and blue before."

"We've got an old saying here: '*You don't like the weather in Scotland? Wait five minutes!*' You'll see, you'll get used to it and after a while you won't even feel the rain anymore," Alex added.

"So where are you from Anne?" William asked.

"From Aix-en-Provence. It's in the South of France. Well, from a little village right next to Aix actually."

The steam coming from our cups of tea mixed with the cigarette smoke.

"Mathieu said you came to get a job here, right?"

"Right, I'd like to work for a couple of months for a change of scenery, you could say. I've got some money saved up, so I can take my time, but the goal isn't for me to go back home broke after a gap year!"

"Glad you're here."

My English was far from fluent, but I was able to talk for a good while, before going up to my room, telling them I was exhausted by the trip. Which wasn't a lie: I was tired. As a matter of fact, I still wasn't at ease, and I didn't want them to be asking me why I'd decided to come to this town.

I went into the bathroom. A nice hot shower before slipping into bed would help me sleep. The faucets were really old and hard to turn. The rejuvenating water finally started to flow, and after having washed off traces of my trip, I went to bed without eating.

— CHAPTER TWO —

The very first week I was in Scotland one of my "bucket list" dreams came true: I toured Edinburgh. And I was enchanted by the city. The Edinburgh Castle was like a mountain right in the middle of the town, leaving me speechless. Wandering down a narrow street in the fog, I came across a man wearing a kilt and playing the bagpipes, charming passersby with typical Celtic tunes. I had lunch in one of the pubs on the Royal Mile and chose their local dish: haggis, a stuffed sheep's stomach. I walked it off while shopping in Prince's Street, buying a Scottish tartan scarf.

Little by little I got used to living in St Andrews, my new home. I strolled along the North Sea, sometimes during high tide with waves pounding, and sometimes with a tide so low that the sea seemed to have disappeared. I walked to the ruins of the cathedral, through the ancient cemetery and its age-old tombs. Everything was so calm. I ventured out onto the pier next to the port, wind whipping around me. Far away, on the other side of the sea, beyond England, lay France, and with it Guillaume and Lara.

21

I did my shopping at the local Tesco, buying all sorts of things I'd never heard of in France, like cheddar cheese, honey-baked ham, black pudding, peanut butter and lemon curd. I spent my time wandering around the town. While getting used to paying with the British pound by buying Shakespeare second-hand books, my savings were melting like snow on a sunny day.

One day I took a walk around the lake I saw from my window. At the end of the road, behind the house, a little path led to it. Swans and ducks swam out into the lake when I arrived. I squatted down, so I could watch them swimming around when I suddenly noticed a four-leaf clover in the grass. I couldn't believe it! I quickly picked it, sure that it would bring me luck. A waft of sweet hot air blew on me and I shivered.

There was a large wooded area behind the lake, and I decided to explore it. I could hear twigs snapping when I walked, I could smell damp loam and moist herbs. After a few minutes, I reached a big field bordered by a stream. Partridges flew up as I approached, my calves rubbed against ever-present thistles. I was thrilled to have discovered all this right next to where I lived. I was happy, all alone here, outside in the bracing breeze. I hadn't felt that good in a long time.

The afternoon was coming to an end when I got back. I loved my little hike around the lake. I had finally decided to write a few words to Guillaume on a postcard when the door suddenly opened and a group of men rushed into the room.

"Hey, Anne, here are some of my friends from work," Mathieu declared, smiling.

He introduced me to a weird looking man named Donald, who was carrying his diary. There was also Ben, a redheaded Scotsman smoking a pipe, Tom, a tall blond-haired guy with a buzz cut, wearing a cardigan and a hat that Sherlock Holmes wouldn't have been ashamed of, and Heinrich, a German with small, round glasses. Alex brought some beers into the living room and I joined them. They were all speaking so quickly that I didn't understand a word. I tried to talk to Ben; he had me repeat my sentences several times, he didn't understand me either.

"Too much o' a French accent."

I smiled. It was like a deaf man's dialogue! I'd never even imagined that others wouldn't understand me. He had a thick accent too. He rolled his "r's" so much that it was funny.

Tom asked me:

"So, do you like Lochan Wynd?"

"It's nice. A charming little place."

"Did you go down to the lake?"

"Actually yes, this afternoon."

"Watch out. That place is full of dark stories..."

I had no idea what he could be talking about for such a beautiful little lake. Mathieu interrupted us.

"You've been here for a week already, and I'm sure that you

haven't even had a beer at the pub! That's a sacrilege. Come on, we'll take you!"

The men persuaded me, I followed them. It was warmly decorated inside: thick carpets, painted designs on the ceiling, nice lamps, huge mirrors on the walls and bookshelves at the back of the pub next to a fireplace. The waiter looked at me with interest. I went up to the counter.

"A whisky on ice for the little lady," he said, giving me my drink and winking.

"Thanks."

"You're French?"

"Can you tell?"

"Yup. French accents are charming."

I started to blush, though I understood later that he wasn't trying to flirt with me.

"You're on holiday then?"

"Not really, well a bit, actually. I came to unwind, but I want to get a job. My spare cash won't last forever."

"Sure. So, what are you looking for?"

"I don't know yet."

"Well, come back and see me, we might be hiring soon. Our waitress is leaving."

With his head he indicated a young lady wiping off the tables. She was extremely pregnant. I suddenly felt uncomfortable. Lara. Don't think of her... I grabbed my glass and sat down with the boys.

The conversation around the table had several English and Scottish accents and I tried to follow it. They talked about philosophy, cultural differences, trips they'd taken, films they'd seen. To punctuate our words, we all drank huge amounts of beer and whisky. I ended up drunk, not just with alcohol, but also with music, partying, it had been such a long time for me, I hadn't even been able to listen to the radio.

The pub closed for the evening. I went back to 7 Lochan Wynd with my new friends. Mathieu was a small guy, proud to have been born in France. His tousled brown hair almost made him look like Einstein. The front door wasn't locked. That surprised me, but Mathieu explained that they always left it open. I started to ask why, but he had already gone to get a bottle of wine. I sat down on the front steps, with Alex and William. Mathieu soon came back.

"This stuff is terrible!" I exclaimed, after taking a sip from the glass he'd given me.

"I know, Anne, but we're not in France now. That's the best you can get here."

I continued in English so that William and Alex could understand. Drinking wine helped words to flow. For me speaking English was something quite exotic; it made me feel as if I'd forgotten what had happened to me in my French life.

Nevertheless, I was frustrated to find it so terribly difficult to talk in this new language. Everything was cluttered up in my head. When I wanted to say a word in English, my vocabulary was lacking, and all I could express were trivial things. William said I spoke like a book, in an academic way.

It was getting late, and I decided to go to bed. Alex grabbed me by the arm as I passed him.

"Don't lock your door."

I had a strange dream that night, still wondering about it when I woke up. I was walking on a lake, naked, seeing white clouds reflected beneath my feet. I had long blond hair and was very pale. I could feel someone behind me, but when I turned around, all I could discern were the trees. I leaned down. My hair grew and touched the water. At that very moment I became translucent, then liquid, then melted into the lake. I could no longer get out of the water, but could make out people walking near the woods, looking for me, even if they couldn't find me. My hair was floating in front of my eyes. I could feel the weight of the water on me. Someone suddenly took me by the hand, and I turned around to see Lara, who was four or five. She was smiling at me.

I woke up sweating. My mouth was dry, my heart was pounding. I didn't recognize my room. Where was I? After a few seconds, I was able to pull myself together and got up, opening the curtains. I could make out the lake in the thick fog, shadows of the surrounding trees were reflected on it.

I needed some fresh air and opened the window. Minute drops of fog moistened my face. That did me good. I could hear the caw of crows, echoing over the lake. The sun hadn't yet risen, although daylight was timidly making its way through the clouds. I suddenly noticed the silhouette of someone walking away from the lake. Who would be standing there at this time of day? Maybe someone coming back after a night of partying? I squinted: it was a young lady with long hair, wearing a bathrobe. Could she be a sleepwalker? As she continued, I finally could no longer see her. I shut the window and went back to bed, but sleep eluded me and I lay awake. Minutes seemed like hours. Since I'd lost my little girl, time was standing still. Every night, I was waiting for something, but I had no idea what.

I opened *Hamlet* and threw myself into reading, unsuccessfully: the words made no sense to me. All I could hear was my heart beating in my ears.

I remembered how long the nights were after Lara had died. Hearing Guillaume gently snoring and feeling his calm warmth next to me, while I was still cold and unable to rest. How unfair! What was I doing in this unpleasant bed, in this oppressing room, in this insignificant house? We were nothing, living with absurdity until the end of our ridiculous existence. I missed Lara so much! I could feel her, nice and warm in my womb, safe. She didn't weigh much, but it was a discreet presence inside me, an integral part of me. But when I put my hand on my abdomen, it was now empty. Nothing.

"She's a beautiful baby," the midwife had told me. *"Look at those little fingers, her little face..."*

How could I not go mad? She weighed 930 grams, just over two pounds. Her skin was blood red. I hadn't wanted them to inject that product into her, I would have preferred to keep her inside.

"Rock her, she needs you. You're a mother now, despite that. Create a bond with her, accept the fact that she existed and now she's gone."

In the morning I got up and opened the curtains: wild lands, the little lake with its swans, the grass that the gray rabbits nibbled on, the woods in the background. I hadn't slept a lot.

I went down to the kitchen, wearing my pj's, my head still heavy and my thoughts still unclear.

"Breakfast is ready!"

Mathieu and William were seated at the kitchen table. I could smell freshly fried bacon. They'd also made scrambled eggs, porridge, and pancakes, without forgetting boxes of cereal. A feast! There was still some coffee left in the coffee pot, and I poured myself a cup, heating it up in the microwave. William was talking, but it was hard to concentrate on what he was saying this early in the morning. It felt like my brain was just as scrambled as the eggs on my plate. I had to switch my French "off" and my English "on."

"Sleep well?"

"Not bad, thanks."

Mathieu and William looked at each other. Mathieu finally started to express what they'd both been thinking.

"Your room... It's been empty for a long time."

"You know that the house belonged to Alex's grandmother, who now lives in an old people's home," William added.

"She is the one who always said not to lock the doors here."

"Plus, it overlooks the lake."

"That's why no one ever rents it."

Surprised, my fork still in my hand, I asked them to explain.

"What do you mean—no one ever rents it? What does that have to do with the room?"

They seemed to hesitate. Then, Mathieu began, in French this time.

"Anne, you're a nice girl, you should know. Some people left this place after having only slept for a night in your room. Too many strange rustle and creepy sounds. We're just worried about you. You've been living in the house for a week already and haven't said a word. Plus, we hardly ever see you around here."

I was dumbfounded.

"That's nice of you, but I didn't hear a thing. What is this, some type of 'hazing' for new renters?"

"Not at all, we're serious here. If everything is fine, that's great."

"I often wake up at night. If there had been something strange, I would have seen it. Where's Alex?"

"He went to church."

"To church?"

He merely shrugged his shoulders as an answer. William left. Mathieu lit up a cigarette and stepped outside to smoke. I finished my breakfast, wondering about all this. I'd have to ask Alex if all this was really true. His grandma's house? Noises at night? Except for my nightmares and insomnia, I was fine. I went up to take a shower and when I walked back down, Mathieu was still there. I joined him on the front porch.

He barely noticed that I'd arrived, he was so busy staring at the window on the second floor across the street.

"Jesus, is she ever beautiful!"

I squinted and looked over, but didn't see anything special. Then, a silhouette appeared through the window, and I understood. The young lady had long straight black hair, with bangs. Her eyes were a sparkling shade of green, with powder white skin and cherry red lips that made her angular face into something particularly luminescent. She could have been sketched by Botticelli. We could hear her laugh, and Mathieu grabbed my wrist.

"She's a goddess. I can't stop thinking about her. She smiled at me yesterday."

"Did you talk to her?"

"No, not yet, I don't know what to say."

A guy with an extravagant hairdo suddenly opened the door across the street. His hair was styled into a huge red and blue Mohawk.

"Hey Mathieu!"

He was wearing a bathrobe and holding a mp3 player with earphones. His head nodded in time with the music he was listening to.

"Hey Pete. How are you?"

"Cool, man. What are you guys doing tonight? See you at the pub?"

"Yeah, maybe," Mathieu answered.

Pete waved at us and walked away.

"Who's that?" I asked.

"Pete. Rebecca's brother."

Rebecca, the Botticelli painting.

"Mathieu?"

"Hmm?"

"I was thinking about what you said, when we were having breakfast. I didn't hear anything last night, but I did see someone."

He turned around.

"You saw someone? In your room?"

"No, not at all. I'm an insomniac, and I didn't sleep a wink last night. So, I got up, peered out the window, and I noticed a shadowy figure walking. I think it was a lady. With long hair."

"You know, a lot of people go there when it's dark. Cheap thrills, to scare themselves. It's pretty grim there."

"But... I went there yesterday and I found it really beautiful. Really pleasant, you know the swans, the daisies, all that."

"Are you kidding? It's just a damp swamp."

Rebecca came back to the window. She was brushing her long dark hair.

Mathieu no longer cared what I said. I left him with his musings and returned inside to spend the rest of the day with mine too.

— CHAPTER THREE —

The next day, when I got up, I was determined to make a serious effort so this trip would actually heal me. Meeting Mathieu's friends and talking with them had triggered something deep inside. It felt like a weight had been taken off my chest. If only this feeling could last forever! I had been so unstable lately that it sometimes surprised even me.

To get off on the right foot, I had to start by looking for a job.

I didn't know what I was searching for, though. One of my friends who left France to work in London told me that it was easy to quickly find well-paid positions in the United Kingdom. I had resigned from my position in Aix with no regrets—I was in charge of the book section in a huge department store. Perhaps I could find a better job here.

I left to get myself a cup of coffee. It was nice out, I sat on the patio in South Street and lit up a cigarette. Job hunting might not be that easy. I thought back to the day when I'd selected this destination. I'd started off by thinking of London. Everyone was going to London, talking about London. But I was apprehensive. This immense megalopolis, a mixture of so many civilizations... I'd never liked big cities, like Paris, I'd never felt at ease there. The only place where I was comfortable in was my little village next to Aix, although I loved Aix City too. I did a technical university degree there when I was younger, that was where I'd met Guillaume. In a nutshell, I didn't want to get lost in some threatening urban jungle but to take time to reflect and heal in a small-town environment. That's why I chose Scotland, a country of dreams, legends and mysteries. That's how I discovered the breathtaking landscapes in the Isle of Skye (too insular), the Highlands (too isolated), Dundee (still too big), and finally ended up on the East Coast with St Andrews. Bingo. A place with the best of both worlds, the sea and wind, history and local heritage, and cute cobbled streets.

With hindsight, however, I wondered if I shouldn't have traveled to London instead. It would have been easier to find a job there. The larger the city, the more opportunities, no? It occurred to me that it wasn't too late, I could still leave and go there if I wanted to. I was free. Truly free, something I realized for the very first time.

"Hi!"

Someone walked in front of me, putting an end to this line of thought. Suddenly the patio, the pedestrian street, the cigarette, everything was back to normal.

"Can I sit down?"

It was Alex.

"Sure, sorry. I was daydreaming."

"I could take a coffee too."

He put his backpack down on a chair, next to his books, and asked the waiter for a coffee.

"Did you just get out of class?"

"That's right, it was Classic English Lit from the 19th century. You know, Emily Brontë and those guys."

"Sure. *Wuthering Heights*, is that it?"

"Spot on! Did you read it?"

"No, but I remember that the book sold a lot in our store."

"You work in a bookstore?"

"I used to, but I resigned so I could leave. I don't know if it was a good idea. It doesn't look like it will be easy to find a job here."

The waiter brought him a steaming espresso. I finished mine.

"I guess it depends on what you're looking for. Do you like it here? Do you miss France?" Alex asked.

"Not too much. Except for the cheese and sausages, of course!"

"Yuk! Everything I hate. What about your family? Mathieu said you were engaged. Do you have any kids?"

My stomach knotted up. Like someone was choking me from inside and I could no longer breathe. I had to control myself not to cry. When would it end?

"Something wrong? You're white as a ghost."

I lit up another smoke. I had to master my emotions. After a couple of puffs, I felt better.

"I'm fine. I'll walk a bit."

"I have to go to the library to pick up some books. Why don't you come with me?"

We took the narrow road that cut through to North Street. In front of St Salvator's Chapel, I noticed a strange drawing on the sidewalk made from lighter cobblestones.

"What's that?"

"Watch out, make sure you don't step on it!"

Astonished, I quickly moved away.

"How come?"

"You don't know what these two letters stand for?"

I took a closer look and the pattern in the cobblestones did seem to be made up of an intertwined P and H.

"I have no idea. What does PH mean?"

"PH — Patrick Hamilton's initials. He was a Protestant university professor and a martyr right here during the Scottish Reformation. If you walk on his initials, you'll never graduate."

"But I'm not a student."

"You never know, it still could bring you bad luck. You're looking for a job, right?"

That convinced me and I made sure I didn't step on any PH cobblestones. We arrived at the library.

Its facade was covered with wooden beams, like an old store. While Alex went in, I stayed outside to read what was posted. There were advertisements about upcoming events, the sale of various objects, mostly for schoolbooks.

Then, one caught my eye.

Assistant University Librarian

Temporary Job

We are looking for a librarian who is enthusiastic about supporting information literacy development to work at our library. IT skills required; duties would include involvement in the day-to-day running of the library.

Just what I needed, at least to begin. I ripped the job offer off the wall and put it in my pocket, then walked back home, in a good mood, to tweak my resume. Maybe avoiding those PH cobblestones did bring me luck.

A few days later, I started my new position. I'd still be having a lot of time off, though. It was only a contract for two hours per day, for a month. Yet, I took it, as that opened the door for me there in Scotland, allowing me to wait until I found something better. I had to remain at the service of the students, do their photocopies, tell them whether a book was available or not, put books back on the shelves, basic stuff like that. The library had four stories and an interminable number of shelves. Easy to get lost there. It was calm and everyone whispered. I found old leather-bound books, but also books from all over the world, in many languages. I wanted to read them all.

When I left, I suddenly felt like sharing my enthusiasm with Guillaume. I took my phone out.

"Anne, finally! How are things going?"

I was both moved and invigorated when I heard his voice. I could speak in my own language without having to think about each word!

"Not bad. It was a bit tough when I first got here, but I just landed a little job, that'll help me out."

"Really? Where?"

"In a library. Actually, it's not as interesting as I'd hoped. Plus, it's only for ten hours a week."

"You'll have to search for a better position. That's not going to cover your room and board."

"I know. But for a real job there's lots of paperwork. I'll find something, though."

"Do you like it there? I mean, no regrets for having left?"

"No, no regrets. I think it was the right thing to do. Here, I meet people, I see different things and the landscapes are beautiful. I don't talk about what happened, I mean that my past isn't a burden here. I don't have to keep on pretending or answering questions that make me uncomfortable. You have no idea how much better that makes me feel! What about you? How are you?"

"I miss you. I have trouble falling asleep at night because you're not there. But I'm happy for you."

"I miss you too. I think about you all the time. And about Lara too..."

He didn't answer and I could tell he was uneasy about what I'd just said. I shouldn't have mentioned that.

"When are you planning on coming back?" he asked after a short time.

"I don't know. When are you coming to visit me?"

"Anne, you know it's not easy for me. I'd prefer to have you back at home, so we can get on with our lives, like before."

"I need some time. I really needed a break like this. You see? I've always wanted to discover Scotland. And I love their accent! It's doing me a load of good to be here. I want to find myself another job, get to know the spirit of the town, and become a new person. Or should I say become myself once again."

"Okay. Take your time then, but don't forget I can't wait till you come back. Love you."

"Love you too."

"See you soon?"

"See you soon. Bye."

"Bye sweetie. Take care."

I strangely felt that the distance between us had brought us closer. Now that I'd phoned him, I missed him even more. I wanted to see his face, touch his hands, kiss him. I sighed. Had it really been a good idea to leave? Would I make the three months I'd planned without seeing Guillaume? I had hoped he'd tell me he'd soon be coming to visit me. I know that none of this was logical here: I was the one who had left to allow our couple to take a break. Distancing myself to test my feelings I had for him and the ability I had to get myself back on track: that was what I wanted to do. When I returned, I'd be stronger, our couple would be stronger.

I had arrived in front of a golf course, as far as the eye could see. I could make out the slopes on the course that led right to the ocean, two lovers separated by a sand sheet. The majestic Royal and Ancient Golf Club building that I knew housed one of the world's oldest golf clubs, stood in front of me like a sentinel. A few players were on the course, scattered here and there, nearly invisible white dots. Wind was blowing my hair about, I let my eyes cry. Was it the wind or nostalgia? Probably a bit of both. I stayed there for a while, admiring the landscape and calming myself down, then set off for the town center.

I loved to explore the city in smells. When I took the narrow

Union Street Road to go to Market Street, the smell of hot chocolate from PM Cafe filled the air. Then, I walked past a Subway sandwich shop and I caught a whiff of tempting fries. A bit further on, as I breathed in the sweet scent of cinnamon, I stopped. I had arrived in front of the Christmas shop, with its beautiful shop windows, where I'd bought my figurines. I loved this little store and stepped in. I remembered the old lady who had told me "In Scotland we still believe in legends," and I must admit I was starting to believe her after all these stories of Protestant martyrs and commemorative stones. Things had changed place and I couldn't find the shelf where the fairies and elves used to be.

The shop assistant walked up to me.

"Hi. Don't you sell figurines anymore?"

"Figurines? We've got Santa Claus, reindeer, and..."

"No," I said, cutting her off in the middle of her sentence, "I meant the figurines that were on this shelf here. I bought two cute little fairies."

"Sorry Ma'am, we don't sell figurines like that. Our store only sells Christmas decorations and decorations for special events."

"And does that old lady still work here?"

"You must be mixing us up with another store."

I left, astonished. I didn't think I'd made a mistake, but who knew. All my sleepless nights had made me exhausted and I didn't feel like I usually did during the day.

I joined William at East Sands. He was a nice guy to talk to for two reasons: I learned a lot from him and I was forced to speak English. Our walk led us to the castle in front of the sea. It was a superb ruin built on a rocky promontory, with a Scottish flag waving in the wind. We leaned on the fence to admire the view. William continued his history course for me.

"See the flag, it's a white saltire on a blue background. It represents Saint Andrew's cross, the one he was crucified on. According to legends, a long time ago, the king of Scotland prayed to Saint Andrew for help during a battle between Scotland and Italy. All of a sudden, a strange cloud that looked like a saltire appeared in the clear blue sky. That scared the Italians and encouraged the Scots, who won the battle. They then made Saint Andrew their patron saint."

"So that's how the town came to be called St Andrews?"

"Almost. There's another legend that explains that. They say that Saint Rule brought Saint Andrew's relics back from Greece and he had a shipwreck here, and that's where he founded the city of St Andrews."

"How do you know all this stuff?"

"I took a tour when I first came here and I like history. Speaking of which, I want to show you something else. Alex told me he showed you the PH set in stone."

He took me to the front of the castle and pointed to the ground. You could make out the initials G and W, made from lighter colored cobblestones, almost like mosaics. Those letters reminded me of others: the P and H of Patrick Hamilton. This slab honored the memory of George Wishart, another Protestant martyr who was also burned at the stake. It was hard for me to imagine that people had been killed so violently there, in this calm little town. We went on walking, around the cathedral, to the little pedestrian road leading to the port. I liked this place. I remembered the first time I'd come here, three weeks ago. Time really flew by!

I observed:

"Too bad that this cathedral is now only ruins. It must have been beautiful before."

"You know, the inhabitants of St Andrews were the ones who destroyed it, after John Knox's sermons, explained William. You never read *The History of St Andrews*? It's in the living room, you have to take a look at it. John Knox, a Protestant, preached against Catholicism. He persuaded his church members to sack the cathedral which represented the Pope and Catholicism. After his sermon, that's what they did: they stole everything that was valuable and burned the icons. As of that day, the cathedral was pretty much in ruins and was no longer used as a church. Little by little, the stones were taken to build other buildings."

"The never-ending war between Catholics and Protestants."

We crossed the little bridge and followed a trail that was parallel to the sea. There were gusts of wind and it was hard to gain headway. On one side, lush green grass and the ruins of the cathedral and on the other the huge sand beach and the vast dark blue sea. We continued until we reached the cliffs at the end of East Sands. We saw all St Andrews from there, its rooftops and gray stone houses.

William looked at his watch.

"I didn't realize it was this late! I have to scoot for an appointment with my anthropology prof."

"I don't want you to be late. Thanks for the tour."

"My pleasure. See ya!"

And he waved at me and left. It was a nice place, isolated from the rest of the town, though it overlooked all of it. I sat down on one of the rocks. What a huge and surprising world we lived in. When I left my little village in the south of France, I never thought I'd see so many beautiful things. I took a deep breath of this fresh sea air.

After a long while, I got up and slowly made my way back home. Alex was reading the paper in the living room.

"William told me you had this book, *The History of St Andrews*, can I borrow it? I'd like to learn more about this city's history."

"It's over there, on the shelf."

I walked over to the shelf of books. It wasn't very well organized: there were some books in French, others in English, some old, some new, novels, poetry, dissertations, everything mixed together with some on the right side and others upside down.

"I don't see it."

"It must be in my room then. Let's go get it."

He got up and I followed him. He had photos on the wall too. One of them caught my eye: there was an old lady sitting in a big armchair and Alex, standing behind her, had his arms around her. She seemed to be quite elderly, her face was full of wrinkles, but her eyes were still sparkling.

"That's my grandma."

"The one who owns the house?"

"Right."

"So where does she live now?"

"In an old people's home, in Birmingham, next to my parents. She's in a wheelchair, so it was no longer possible for her to stay in this house, with all these stairs."

"I see. Hey, can you explain to me what's up with my bedroom? I didn't understand if Mathieu was making fun of me or if it was true."

"What did he tell you?"

"That people before me heard noises there. He added I should never lock the door."

He didn't answer right away and sat down, motioning for me to do the same, before continuing.

"Elizabeth, my grandmother, was born in this house and spent her entire life here. Her father was a sailor; he worked on a steamboat that went from Dundee to the north seas to hunt for whales. He was often absent, as the boat remained at sea for long periods of time. Then one day he didn't come back at all. The whaler had been broken by the ice. After this accident, my great-grandmother lost her mind. She talked to herself, spent hours in front of the window. Until this day when she locked my grandma in the room and disappeared. A few days later her body was found in the lake behind the house."

He stopped for an instant.

"After that, my grandmother refused to have any locked doors in this house. She always left them unlocked; it was an obsession for her. I think she was traumatized by having been shut in her room. I respect her choice, and since I've lived here, we never bolt a door, even the front one. Elizabeth stayed here all her life, far from everyone else. She never got married, but late in her life she had my mother. She never told anyone who the father was. Villagers rejected her even more after that."

He stopped again. I didn't know what to say, amazed at what I'd just heard.

"Despite everything, including the death of her parents and gossip in the village, she never left this house. She found work at the laundry and lived alone, raising her daughter—my mother. As strange as that may seem, for her entire life Elizabeth slept in the room overlooking the lake, the one you're in now. Then a few years ago she went to live in an old people's home. When I came to St Andrews to study, I knew that I'd be living here and was looking forward to it. This house is the symbol of my youth:

when I was little, I spent my vacations here and I loved walking on the beach. I've always loved it here, despite it all. It's so beautiful. But I never go down to the lake."

"What about that rustle in the room?"

"When I rented your room out, I could never find anyone who would stay. Even though I never told anyone about this, I think there were rumors in town. Several people have spent the night here, but some of them heard strange sounds, others couldn't sleep because they felt someone was there. I have no idea if it's true or not, I never tried. Mathieu said that you didn't hear anything weird, you didn't feel any strange presences."

"That's true, I didn't hear a thing. But I hardly sleep at all, I'm an insomniac, so I can't blame it on the room."

"That's reassuring then. People are crazy. They must have heard this story, or they wanted to sleep here to see if they could, but then they chickened out and left!"

"You think so?"

"I don't know."

"Do you often go see Elizabeth?"

"Sometimes I go to Birmingham to visit her."

"I'd love to meet her."

"No problem. I'll let you know next time I go. We'll soon be having her ninety-fifth birthday party. So, this is just between us, okay? That's a part of my family's private life. It's Lochan Wynd's 'secret.' Anne, if I didn't tell you about this earlier, it's because I didn't want you to feel uncomfortable here. If you prefer to leave that room, just let me know. Mathieu and William don't have any problems here, but they're not on lakeside."

"I'll tell you that tomorrow then. Anyway, thanks for having told me."

"Sure, and here's the book."

He handed me *The History of St Andrews*.

We suddenly heard crackling sounds outside. Alex and I walked outside onto the front porch. Fireworks. Mathieu was sitting on the steps, and I was about to join him, but then I saw Rebecca next to him. William gestured for me to sit with him.

"What's the celebration?"

"No idea. But who doesn't like fireworks?"

"Right."

They were sparkling in the sky, lighting up my friends' eyes. Then everything went dark again before the sky lit up with multiple colors, with sounds of rockets booming. With the fog, it made me think of a huge fresco reflected in the low clouds.

Then Rebecca stepped back inside and Mathieu joined us.

"What a night... She was so close to me that I could smell the shampoo she used in her hair."

He had lit up a cigarette and was blowing out smoke rings. He handed us a bottle of wine.

"I didn't even finish my bottle. Help yourselves."

We all sat outside, enjoying our cigarettes and drinking wine, while admiring the night.

Alex broke the silence.

"Anne knows."

William and Mathieu both looked at me without a word. Then Alex got up.

"I gotta go, they're waiting for me at the pub. Good night!"

And he slowly walked away.

"So, you didn't lie then, all that stuff about snaps and cracks heard in the room was true."

"We wanted to tell you, but Alex was afraid that it would scare you off."

"You know, we were pretty uncomfortable too when we heard about it, but that didn't stop us. All that happened such a long time ago," William explained.

"That's true. Did you ever sleep in that room?"

"No, the other rooms were vacant, so we didn't want to push our luck."

"Did you hear strange noises?"

"Nothing at all. Except maybe the pipes gurgling."

"Anne, seriously," continued Mathieu, "if you ever need anything, we'll be here. You're strong you know. Forget about what Alex said. Maybe all the rustling in your room is just an old wives' tale, you didn't hear anything anyway."

"You're right. But the fact that this Elizabeth lady slept for her whole life in this room, overlooking her mother's final resting place... It's dreary."

"Elizabeth is sort of peculiar."

"You know her?"

"I met her once. She doesn't talk much, she lives in her own personal world. Rumor has it she's crazy."

"Alex said he'd introduce me to her."

That was the end of this conversation. William had a paper to finish and left. Mathieu hugged me.

"Are you going to be alright? I wouldn't want you to be getting any dark thoughts again. If you ever need me, I'll be here for you."

It wasn't late. The night would be long. Setting off to my room, I thought about the day. The book in the library on all the martyrs in St Andrews, what Alex unexpectedly told me. Something a book could be based on. I wasn't too reassured, especially as I'd already walked down to the lake and had no idea what had happened there. I opened my door. For the first time, I'd be going into Elizabeth's room.

I felt like I was snooping. I'd unwittingly moved into Elizabeth's place. All my stuff was there, though, marking its territory, yet none of it seemed to belong here. I walked up to the window that had attracted me ever since I'd arrived.

What a fantastic view of the lake! This smooth, dark and cold lake. What a contradiction between my first impression and what Alex had just said! I shivered.

Yet, I had to remember that the body of Elizabeth's mother was found there nearly eighty years ago. We couldn't exactly take the lake to court, and it no longer had all those macabre properties, I was sure. At least, I would try to persuade myself of that.

After hearing all this, I needed to take a hot bath. I turned the faucets on to fill the tub, they were still half-stuck and I had to make an effort. The little bathroom quickly steamed up and when I shut the water off, I felt like I was in a Turkish bath. I put one leg into the burning water, then the other, and finally my whole body. I closed my eyes.

It felt so good here. I took a deep breath and put my head under the water. I immediately saw a brief flash of a fetus floating in its mother's womb, in rhythm with its muffled heartbeat. I came up and took another deep breath. Lara would never leave me. I'd have to live with the pain of her loss.

I climbed out and emptied the tub, and wearing only my bathrobe, walked back into my room. It seemed to be unusually bright for this time of the day. I went to the window and saw the moon shining brightly between the clouds. It had a strange amber hue I'd never seen before. This curious color could also be seen in the leaves on the trees, on the lake, in the shadows of the night. Did the Northern Lights shine here? I picked up the pack of cigarettes on my desk when something fell. It was one of the figurines that I'd bought right after arriving. I was sure that I'd put both of them on my bedside table, strange. I picked the one up that had fallen. Luckily, it wasn't broken, but it seemed different. It was now wearing an ocher-colored dress. When I bought them, weren't the dresses purple? I must have been mistaken.

I put the figurines back on my table, lit up a cigarette and opened the window. It was a beautiful evening. I sat down on the windowsill and stayed there for a long time, admiring this sky full of energy and movement, these strange clouds where the stars sometimes peaked through, and this golden and mysterious moon.

— CHAPTER FOUR —

The next day, at lunch, I walked in on William and Alex in the living room, munching on pizzas and vinegar drenched fries. I crashed their lunch break.

"Can I have a piece of pizza?"

"Sure, help yourself!"

While eating I asked them about the strange moon.

"Did you see the moon last night? Like it was on fire, smoky orange-colored..."

"Last night the rum was smoky orange too!"

They burst out laughing.

"How to tell you—last night I didn't notice much of anything. It was *Raisin Weekend*, our student integration weekend," Alex explained to me.

I turned to William.

"I didn't notice anything either. In the fall in the US, there are lots of colored moons that we call 'Harvest Moons', maybe that was it.

"Maybe what we call 'Red Moons' in France.

"Who knows? You work at the library, just look it up!"

"You're right. But I *work* there, I don't have time to read."

Then Mathieu joined us. Wrinkled clothes, white as a sheet, he didn't look like he had fully woken up yet or recovered from last night.

"I just got in. I'm exhausted. Can I have some fries?"

Without waiting for an answer, he took some from Alex's box.

"I'm giving an organ recital today at Saint Trinity Church. Anne, do you want to come?"

"I didn't know you played the organ."

"I started when I was six. It's not that complicated, it's like playing the piano. But I feel like hell... I'd really like it if you came, that would give me a good reason to do a good job."

"Okay. Count me in. What time?"

"At four."

"See you then."

I headed to the library for my two hours of work. It was all quiet, the students were studying in the reading rooms. I put books back on the shelves and cleared the tables off. Sometimes people donated books, I had to label them and put them where they belonged. There was no stress here, not like in the department store I used to work in before.

And a batch of donated books had been delivered earlier. I was lucky. A book quickly caught my attention: it was old and had seen better days, some pages were ripped and part of the text was even illegible. The cover was stained, though it must have been beautiful when new. I delicately opened it and immediately smelled mold and dust. I began reading it.

"*The Reform had begun. Reformed pastors were vehement in their denunciations of corrupt Roman Christians. Reformed faith was sanctioned by the law.*"

Was this book about St Andrews' religious history? I looked at the cover: neither an author's name nor a title. I peered around me, no one in sight, just students busily working. I decided to continue a bit.

"*The first martyr was John Resby, an Englishman who converted to reformed doctrines. Resby preached in the diocese of St Andrews, and his popularity drew the attention of Bishop Wardlaw, who had him imprisoned. With forty charges against him, all accusing him of heresy, Resby was sentenced to be burned at the stake. The court rendered its sentence in Perth, there where he had been the most successful. This was in 1407.*

Paul Craw was next on the persecution list. He came to St Andrews to work as a physicist and zealously preached reformed doctrines. Wardlaw had him thrown in jail and accused him of opposing the Pope's power, thus of heresy. Just like Resby, he was sentenced to death by being burned at the stake and this took place

St Andrews, in 1433, in Market Street."

Burned at the stake in Market Street? This was where I did my shopping! I continued to read, both surprised and intrigued.

"The third martyr in St Andrews was the famous Patrick Hamilton, Abbot of Fern, who died on February 29, 1528. He'd discovered Luther's doctrines in Paris and preached them upon returning to Scotland. When he came to St Andrews and his religious opinions were made public, he was imprisoned in the castle, taken to court, and as he refused to recant, sentenced to death. He was attached to bundles of wood in front of St Salvator Church, which had to be constantly relit because of their humidity and suffered for six hours. This is how the most famous martyrs of the Reform died, at the age of twenty-four."

Twenty-four... Never would I have thought that Patrick Hamilton was so young when I saw the slab with PH on it.

"Rumor has it that when he passed away, the features of his face revealed themselves on a stone in the St Salvator Church clock. For the first time, the crowds of spectators were moved by his sufferance and they began to doubt the logic of the Catholic Church."

This was something I wanted to talk to William about, as he well knew the history of the town. Perhaps he would be aware of the martyr's face on the St Salvator Church Tower. I had gone past that church so many times without looking up.

"Then there was Henry Forrest, five years after Hamilton, in 1533, who had dared to defend him. He had a copy of the New

Testament translated into English (as not preaching in Latin was a sacrilege). He was put to death before being burned at the stake, not to shorten his suffering, but so that spectators would not have to recall Hamilton's agony. Forrest's body was burned at the cathedral's northern gate, so that as few people as possible would see the flames."

How many had died? Would that list ever end? I was surprised that they wrote this about the cathedral, now so calm and relaxing.

"In 1546, George Wishart, a priest who had embraced Jean Calvin's ideas, also became a martyr for having defied the Catholic Church. Crowds flocked in to listen to him preach. Cardinal Beaton imprisoned him in the chateau's dungeon and had him sentenced to death for heresy. The very next day he was taken to a stake in North Street, wearing black linen and attached to bags of gunpowder. Wishart burned to death in a cloud of smoke and explosions, claiming his faith until his dying breath. People say that when he passed, a terrible hurricane came in from the North Sea, destroying several houses and demolishing the grandstands where the spectators had been sitting. They were forced to find refuge in the Cardinal's courtyard.

The last martyr who died in St Andrews was Walter Myln, a priest who no longer gave masses and who was consequently suspected of heresy. He was nearly eighty and could not even walk without assistance to his place of execution. He died in 1558 in front of the cathedral's main entrance, on The Pends.

Roughly thirty other people were accused of heresy. In 1838, the inhabitants of St Andrews decided to build a monument to commemorate the memory of these martyrs who, because of the Reform and its atrocities, perished. The monument can be seen on the western side of The Scores."

A student who needed photocopies from a book on astrophysics interrupted me. I mechanically took her book and placed it on the photocopier, still musing on what I had just read. Such horrible things had taken place here! It gave me the creeps. All of this was true, and I walked in front of it every day. And to think that students avoided stepping on the PH slab, laughing, whereas he'd suffered atrociously. What a barbarian time. Like the Middle Ages, actually.

I gave the girl her book and her photocopies. When I got back to my desk, I couldn't find the old book again. I looked around, but only saw people reading or taking notes. I was disappointed, I would have liked to flip through it a bit more. I finished my work, then took my Assistant Librarian cap off to become Anne once again (two hours went by quickly), and began browsing through history books but couldn't find it. Someone must have borrowed it when my back was turned, and with a bit of luck, they'd soon put it back.

I left and walked down The Scores. The wind was blustery here next to the sea. I quickly noticed the monument in memory of the martyrs. I had often followed this road but obsessed with the majestic golf course and the untamed beauty of the sea, I'd never really taken a close look at this obelisk. I started to read the inscription on the side.

"IN MEMORY OF THE MARTYRS PATRICK HAMILTON, HENRY FORREST, GEORGE WISHART, WALTER MILL, WHO IN SUPPORT OF THE PROTESTANT FAITH, SUFFERED DEATH BY FIRE AT ST ANDREWS BETWEEN THE YEARS 1528 AND 1558. THE RIGHTEOUS SHALL BE IN EVERLASTING REMEMBRANCE."

So the book was true then. These men had been burned at the stake here, in this town, and this was all that remained of them.

I reached Saint Trinity Church, a bit early. Small groups of people were lingering outside, but I didn't find Mathieu: he must have already been inside, rehearsing. I went in. The huge and beautifully decorated church was lit by dozens of candles. It housed many antiques: sculpted chairs, large paintings, a wooden seat engraved with the coat of arms of Mary of Scotland. Then I saw another object in the showcase window that really gave me a chill: a tongue shear. I read the informative note: "instrument to punish blasphemers." And to think they used it! I preferred not even to go there and admire the organ: it was stunning with its long metallic cylinders. However, I still couldn't see Mathieu.

I took a place on the right, in the last row. I could make out the wooden pulpit and stained-glass windows behind it. People began to sit down. I could hear them whispering. It seemed they were looking at me though and I felt uncomfortable. A man dressed in a long black tunic slowly walked in front of me, holding a big pendulum. What could he be doing? His hand was scarred, his nails long and filthy, and I couldn't stop myself from staring at the golden pendulum he was swaying back and forth, faster and faster.

I suddenly heard some powerful notes, startling me: the recital was beginning. The man in black put his pendulum into his sleeve and walked away.

"Good evening everyone. Tonight, to start, I'll be playing *La Toccata* by Bach."

I recognized Mathieu's voice. The first musical notes filled the church with their infinite sadness and their dominating power. I was so stirred that my entire body began to shiver. What an intense piece! I felt like the notes were going inside me, right to my heart. I pictured Mathieu's fingers gliding quickly over the keys, his back curved, his head nodding in rhythm with the most powerful notes. This little guy, sitting on his wooden seat, shattering the sacred silence of this church, with each and every person listening to him play. At the end of the day, an organ in a church could be frightening. It seemed to be a bit arrogant to be sitting alone behind this huge musical instrument, perched high above everyone else in a church, like God.

While listening to him play, I peered around. I noticed one column head in particular: sculptures representing men and women at the stake, agonizing. Assassinating flames, tortured bodies, hands begging... I could imagine them screaming in pain, grimaces of those dying. I looked away and suddenly seemed to see a strange pale face in the church, with sunken eyes and a mouth wide open as if it was shouting. My heart skipped a beat and I averted my gaze, but I remained consumed by this vision and shivered. I even thought I heard a long death rattle. People turned at me. Why were they all staring? I was ready to leave. The music continued, more violent, more macabre. The candles flickered, some even went out, and I was suddenly freezing. I could see strange shadows on the wall. The piece was finally over, followed by a short instant of silence, then applause.

"Sonata for Piano Number 14, called *Clair de Lune*, by Beethoven."

The music started back up, even sadder and more melancholic, with higher notes. This piece made me think of solitude and loss of a loved one. Something I knew only too well. *Clair de Lune*, those empty nights I spent waiting, firstly so that Lara would come back, then to finally rest and sleep. Lara, who for everyone else, had never really existed, as she was never really born; thus she had never really passed away, except for me. Tears welled up in my eyes, I couldn't stop one from running down my cheek. This melody touched me right in my heart, ripping me apart. I thought about our heartache, about Guillaume and myself, because he too had suffered, perhaps not in the same way I did, but in his way, even if I'd often accused him of the opposite. He must have tried to mask his pain to help me overcome mine, to continue living. I'd always begrudged him whereas he'd made his utmost to support me. And now I was far from him. How long would he wait for me? Would I lose him too?

Silence. Applause.

"And to finish this concert, *Variations de Goldberg* by Bach."

I wiped my tears with my sleeve. This last piece was lighter and more tender. Almost like a romantic song from the Middle Ages. That calmed me, I let myself be lulled by the music until it ended. After I'd lost Lara, I couldn't stand listening to music anymore—it seemed to be indecent and not in phase with my feelings. Music was beautiful though...

A thunder of applause broke the silence. The spectators got up and looked at me while continuing to applaud. In fact, they just all wanted to thank the person who had played the organ, who was just behind me, and I turned around too. Mathieu was standing there, he bowed and disappeared.

We met up outside a bit later.

"Did you like it?"

"It was incredible! I was overwhelmed."

"Thanks."

"And what an astonishing church. Listening to you play in this environment was heavenly!"

"You're doing puns now! But yes, you're right, the church is beautiful. It's ancient, it has its history. Let me get you something to drink."

When we were together, we spoke French, it was so much easier to express complicated ideas. Once we sat down on the velvet chair in one of the corners of the dimly lit pub, both enjoying a cold beer, we started to talk. From History with a capital H, we began to tell each other personal stories.

Mathieu confided to me about the nights he spent drinking and writing frantically. I replied that I often couldn't sleep at night either, and I confessed my secrets to him: Lara, my insomnia and my depression.

"The piece that you played tonight brought back so many emotions that I'd been trying to bury..."

I confided in him my deepest secrets, and that did me a world of good to be able to actually release myself from this story. Before, it would have been too hard to talk to someone about my pain. But I felt that now I was starting to accept it and live with it, that I could finally share it.

He had taken my hand and was listening to me carefully. I could see he was moved by what I had told him. His simple presence was comforting me. I needed so much to talk to someone, to stop these thoughts from continuously haunting me... He suddenly opened his mouth.

"You know, right from the very beginning I knew you were hiding something. Now, I understand much better. Like me, you lost someone you loved. I know that what happened to us is different, but I commiserate with you. I lost my little sister when she was only 13. Run over by a car. Since then, I have to live with this unceasing pain, buried deep down inside of me, but I try to control it, to exteriorize it, for example, by playing the piano or organ. You never forget, all you can do is try to live with it in the course of time."

Night was already falling. The stars were starting to twinkle when they broke through the clouds, and a bit of drizzle made the air damp. The roads, the darkness, the street lights, everything was wrapped in this cool cocoon. The town seemed to be sleeping, but I knew this wasn't true: behind the doors in the pubs, glasses of beer were being raised, behind the windows in houses, people were watching TV. Behind all these walls, life went on. We cut across the lawn to Lochan Wynd. I could make out bright eyes on the grass, and when they heard us, rabbits scampered away. The front door wasn't locked.

I went into my little room and turned on the TV, just for some background noise. Whatever was on, I liked to hear English being spoken.

I ordered some fish and chips and powered up my laptop. Guillaume was online. I quickly began to talk to him via the chat. At the same time, I opened several job-hunting sites. If I applied to a few every day, I'd finally find myself a real job. The "Guillaume" window flicked on in orange.

"Honey! Is everything alright?"

"Sure, I'm pretty well settled in now and I think I'm doing better."

"Really? I'm happy for you. I was so worried for you."

"There's something different here. Something in the people, their good moods, how nice they all are. And I even told someone about Lara today."

"Nice, who did you tell?"

"Mathieu, my French friend. Words were spewing from my mouth uncontrollably. And while I was speaking, instead of being uncomfortable, I felt freed."

"That's a good sign, I'm sure it means you're accepting it. You know, your parents asked me for some news. Maybe you should call them. Or email them."

"I don't know if I'm ready. Not yet."

"I gave them your address. I hope that was okay?"

"Of course."

"Okay. How about at night? Can you sleep?"

"Not really. When I finally fall asleep, I often have nightmares. It's exhausting."

"It must be. But darling, it won't last forever you know."

Someone knocked. It was the delivery guy: my meal was piping hot, in its cardboard box. I gave him five pounds and thanked him.

I came back to my computer.

"What about your library job?"

"I'll be finishing it next week. But it wasn't because of my job that I'm feeling better. It's because of the people I've met."

"Anne, I'm not kidding here, I miss you. Come back soon."

"I miss you too. Why don't you come and visit me, you'd understand why I like it so much here! So many incredible things happened in this little town. This afternoon I saw the monument for Protestant martyrs: five of them were burned at the stake right here in St Andrews, can you believe that?"

"You were always a history buff. You and this town were made for each other! And I'm sure you haven't learned everything yet. That's cool, something that interests you. Tell me, you'll be back for Christmas, won't you? Try to have a look at tickets back. When you book early, they're often much cheaper."

"I promise I'll look. Love you."

"Love you too."

"Bye Sweetie."

"Bye Hun."

I actually did like the distance between us now, as it allowed me to erase the tragedy that linked us. Our relationship was more peaceful, I was no longer bitter. As we didn't talk to each other every day, each conversation was important and made me happy. Though I didn't want to admit it, I missed my parents too. Now that I was a bit reconciled with myself, as I'd started to go out again, I wanted to make up with them too. I checked out the airlines and compulsively bought a ticket back to France for December 20th. I had a date now.

Then I looked at the job offers, while munching on my fish and chips. There wasn't much right in St Andrews. In a little town like this, it wasn't surprising. I sighed and gave up. I'd print off some resumes and drop them off in places where I wouldn't mind working, that would be more useful.

I finished eating and wiped my hands on the already greasy napkin, then lit a cigarette and opened the window to smoke. It was already much cooler, and a light fog was settling in. I'd given up smoking when I'd known I was pregnant, but after I lost Lara, I started back up again. After all, you needed some pleasures in life. Besides, smoking had really helped me. Thanks to a simple cigarette, I was able to remain composed during arguments, smoking calmed me down, it was like a friend during all that time I was so terribly alone.

I put on my nightgown after having glanced at my baby's photo inside my closet—that's how I bid her goodnight—and went to bed. When I lay down, the sheets were cold and I couldn't close my eyes. I couldn't stop myself from thinking of the lady who died in the lake I saw from my window. I turned the lights back on and powered up my laptop. Words that described the martyr that these men endured danced in front of my eyes. I came across portraits of Patrick Hamilton in Google Images. Lithographs of an ascetic looking man, dressed in black with a white collar, a small beard and upturned mustache, but with tender eyes. I read several more stories about all the martyrs in St Andrews, then about the history of the town. What I learned matched what I'd found out in the library but had fewer details. They often strangled the Protestant martyrs before burning them so they wouldn't suffer. I thought about Joan of

Arc, who also perished because of her beliefs. Did she suffer too?

I looked at my clock: 2:34. My eyelids were starting to tingle, as if I had sand in them. I rubbed my eyes. As I was reading one last article, I saw a reflection on the screen. Briefly but clearly. A distorted face, with a huge forehead and black eyes that were close to each other. I was startled and moved away from my laptop, bringing my hand to my mouth to smother a scream. My heart was pounding. But the reflection had disappeared. My fatigue was playing tricks on me. I sighed and turned my laptop off.

As soon as I came back to bed, I smelled a very unpleasant whiff of something burning. I opened my door and went into the hall, but it was fainter there, it smelled worse in my room. I didn't have any dangerous devices. I examined all over to see where it could be coming from but didn't find anything. It perhaps came from my laptop, maybe a problem with its ventilation. I opened the window to air out the room. Outside, I could see two silhouettes in the mist. They weren't moving. My hands shaking, I closed the window and went downstairs to read.

I finally fell asleep at 4:00, my forehead on my open book.

— CHAPTER FIVE —

Things weren't like they'd been before. All I could think about was Lochan Wynd's secret. Since I'd found out, it was like I was living with the knowledge of the truth and ambivalence of everything. I was no longer alone in my room, there were now two of us, Elizabeth and I, both going about our business, her in the past, and me in the present. I knew that the lake had been a terrifying place and that it was now a pleasant one. I knew that the sea was beautiful, but that it could also take lives. She had lost her mother, I had lost my daughter.

We were now in the middle of autumn. With the end of daylight-saving time and the cold weather coming, days were shorter and it got dark earlier and earlier. Birds had started to migrate; I saw them flying to the sea. The leaves had turned and begun to fall.

It was my last week as an assistant librarian. This job had regulated my days for a month, but except for having earned a few pounds, it didn't bring me anything.

On my last day, I thanked my colleagues for everything, gave my uniform back, picked up my last pay slip and left.

I was disappointed that I hadn't found that old book again in the library, I had even begun to think that I'd imagined it. I'd looked for it, but to no avail. In its place I had *The History of St Andrews*, a little book about the town from its beginnings until now. This confirmed my view that my spirit was open to both what was happening now, and what had taken place in the past. When I walked through St Andrews, with every step I took, I could remember what had taken place there.

I'd learned a lot of things in the book, in particular key dates in its history. I was astonished that St Andrews was so old: the foundations of the city dated back to 1140. In the sixteenth century, it had a population of four thousand, including seventy-two bakers. Everyone must have spent their time eating bread! Thanks to its maritime commerce, the town was prosperous, before declining in the eighteenth century, with only three thousand inhabitants and six bakers. In the nineteenth century, it was linked to the rest of the country by a railway, seaside resorts became popular, and with its successful golf course, the city began to flourish again.

A few days after I'd finished my job, I was getting bored. When I saw Mathieu leave in the morning for school, followed by Alex, I realized I no longer had any goals in my days. Up until now though, this trip had done me a world of good, I'd felt much less depressed, finally admitting to myself that I had been. But I needed to work to occupy my mind.

The following night, once again, I barely shut my eyes. I had another nightmare, one I'd never had before. I dreamed that in the midst of a crisis, I stabbed myself in the stomach with a pair of scissors, several times. I suddenly woke up, with a sharp pain in my lower abdomen, and couldn't fall back to sleep and had to patiently wait until sunrise.

I was getting up later and later. I had all the time in the world, no one was waiting for me. I often spent an hour in the shower, two hours in the tub, or even the afternoon in bed. I skipped meals. Sometimes I played chess or cards with William. I spent hours talking to Mathieu. He lent me books that I devoured. Little by little, I was sliding down a slippery slope. I didn't want anything, I felt alone and empty. My life was empty. Everyone I knew was building theirs, but not me. I was stuck in a rut: no job, no goal, no changes. And all these thoughts running through my head, times when I was happy before... Nothing was happening now, I wasn't doing anything, I was no one.

It was Halloween Night. Alex had organized a big Halloween party and had invited lots of people. We all had to wear a costume. I wasn't really used to this as I'd never really celebrated Halloween. What we did back in France, was on All Saints' Day, we went down to the cemetery to flower the graves of those we'd lost. Not a celebration, a sad day, dedicated to the memory of those who were dead. Each year my mom and I put flowers on our family's tombs.

Lara had also left us. She was the one I had to pay homage to this year, so that she'd never be forgotten. But how, with no urn, no grave, nothing? She didn't have anything. There were no traces of her, except in my memory, and on that photo taken the day after labor was induced. She was so tiny, so fragile, had such delicate little features. Her peaceful face made her look like she was sleeping, but the bluish dark circles under her eyes reminded me that she was dead. This photo was the proof that Lara had existed. I gave it a light kiss. I missed my parents, Guillaume, they were so far away. I had lost them all, lost my entire family.

I used my sleeve to wipe away my tears before putting the picture back up in my closet. Then I went out to find myself a costume, although my heart wasn't ready to celebrate. I decided to buy a simple pointed witch's hat and a long black wig, with a little makeup, that would do the trick. I also got some candles and incense. The cashier number two lady was in a good mood.

"Good afternoon, how are you?"

I knew that this was just to be polite, but this time I felt like answering that I wasn't fine at all, that I wanted to cry, how did she think someone would be after their baby's passing, just to see her reaction. Despite that, I didn't reply, just smiled, paid and left with my purchases in a bag, without a comment on the cashier's ridiculous costume, a pumpkin hat, before she said, "Happy Halloween!" to me.

Before heading back home, I strolled around the cathedral, still magnificent despite its ruins. I went into the cemetery.

There were loads of old tombs, moss growing on the stones. It had actually become a huge garden with tombstones raised here and there. I walked silently, thinking of those buried there.

The tombstones were engraved, but many of them were so old I couldn't make out what was written. In front of me, Henry Sword's epitaph dated 1662. I kept on, wanting to know more about those buried here, beneath my feet. As I could read, John Duncan Laird was an honest man with a myriad of qualities, well known in St Andrews. He'd died on September 21, 1711. Mary Lion Campbell was good-natured, prudish, and modest. She had passed away in 1829, when she was only 29.

The tombstones all were shaped differently. Some of them were large, some with very detailed Celtic crosses. Others were small and much simpler, some square, others curved on top, or ogive shaped. They all were different, as must have been the personalities of those buried below them. I kept on walking, went under the arches, and saw a young lady dressed in white, with a small book in her hand, looking at me. I smiled at her, but she didn't smile back. It was starting to get dark and the tombstones now began to look like a crowd of people waiting for someone to visit them. The inscriptions on them had not changed in ages. Something was holding me back here, like a duty or task I had to accomplish. While I slowly walked to the exit, on the North Sea side, I saw a stone engraved with ancient characters, flush with the ground, and read it.

"OFTEN I STOOD AS YOU STAND NOW,
TO VIEW THE DEAD, AS YOU DO TO ME.
ERE LONG, AND YOU SHALL BE AS LOW,
AND OTHERS STAND, AND LOOK ON THEE."

This epitaph on Ann Herd's tomb felt like it was calling me. The past of those who'd disappeared was intruding into my present. Before they passed away, all these dead people had spoken, laughed, eaten, had ideas, habits, a physical presence. And now, no one remembered them at all. Like no one remembered Lara.

I walked up to one of the little side doors leading to the cathedral. The young lady dressed in white was kneeling on a tomb, with her head bowed. She must have been there most of the afternoon. Night would be falling soon. I'd have to hurry. I left, passed by the ruins of St Mary on the Rock, and arrived to the pier in the port, just a bit further. The wind had picked up, I could feel ocean spray on my face. I walked up to the end, it was getting narrower and narrower, as the sea was rising over the stones. This was the right place.

Fighting the wind, I lit all the candles I'd purchased, trying to protect them so they wouldn't go out. I also lit three incense sticks, holding them in my hands. They were immediately consumed. Some of the candles were snuffed by the wind. I patiently lit them back up, also lit up all the rest of the incense, kneeled down and closed my eyes. I thought of Lara. I remembered her profile perfectly and could have drawn it without looking at the photo.

"My darling little baby, I'm so sorry you passed away, you didn't make it. I never stop thinking of you, I'll never forget you. You'll always be in my souvenirs. I miss you so much."

Then I thought about everyone in my family who'd gone... Gramps with his fat stomach, my other grandfather with his wooden leg, my great-grandmother who always sat in her armchair, Granny in her garden, surrounded by flowers. They'd always be there too for me; I'd never forget them.

I opened my eyes. The smoke from the incense looked like tiny moving figures, dancing in the wind. Then a stronger gust put all the candles out at once. I threw the consumed incense sticks into the sea and picked up the candles. My hands were frozen.

I barely recognized N° 7 Lochan Wynd when I got back! Alex had outdone himself with the decoration: candles, pumpkins, spiderwebs all over. And I didn't recognize my friends or roommates either. All I saw were people dressed as vampires, skeletons, a guy with an axe coming out of his head and many devils with long tails. The loud music was making my eardrums vibrate. The noise in the living room was infernal, people laughing, speaking, the music, and I nearly tripped over a drink in an abandoned glass someone had put down in an unexpected place. I ran upstairs to put my costume on. I looked at my reflection in the mirror before going back down: I'd have to change my attitude. No way was I going to seem moody or unhappy tonight. I put more eyeliner on and drew a huge wart on my nose. After having put the wig on, a black dress, and a witch's hat, I was finally ready and went back down into that inferno.

"Anne! You little witch!"

It was Mathieu. He had pointed vampires teeth and a white and nearly feminine face.

"Come with me. Donald and Ben over there have been asking about you."

I followed him. Donald. Yup, he still was carrying his diary. And Ben, the redhead. They were talking to William, who was carrying a huge branch.

"Come on, tell us."

"Maybe Che Guevara or Rasputin. Just saying their names excites me. Or Patrick Hamilton if I have to choose some historic character."

Hamilton. The most famous Scottish martyr. Now I knew who he was. I butted in.

"What are you guys talking about?"

"Donald wanted to know who we'd like to meet if we could bring someone from the past back."

"For me," Mathieu answered, "it would be the child genius, Mozart, or Van Gogh, the disturbed genius of painting, and the Father of us all, Jesus. What about you, Anne?"

"Let me think... For me, famous authors, like Shakespeare. And my family's ancestors too, or people I don't even know, like those buried in the cathedral's cemetery."

"You're right, they've got old tombstones there. People say that Tommy Morris is buried there."

"Who the heck is Tommy Morris?"

"The famous golfer! Ye know that St Andrews is the home o' golf. Tom Morris Jr. was the world champ when he was only 17!" Ben explained.

"The Open is in July, isn't it?" William interjected.

"Right. Ye dinnae want to miss that!"

I examined William, surprised by his outfit.

"What are you doing with that branch?" I asked.

"That's my costume! Can't you see that I'm disguised as a tree?"

"Sure..."

What a funny idea!

Mathieu walked up with a bottle of whisky and began pouring it, before leaving again.

I had a nice chat with Donald.

"So, do you like Scotland? And St Andrews?" he took over.

"It's a pretty little town. And a historical one too, I read the stories about the Protestant martyrs. It's crazy that all that stuff happened here."

"I heard you went to the cathedral's cemetery."

He smiled wryly at Ben, then asked me:

"Do you like ghost stories?"

He continued to speak without waiting for an answer.

"People say that a White Lady can sometimes be seen there."

"A lady in white?"

"Yeah, a young lady wearing a long pale dress and a veil. Some of us have seen her. She usually appears at sunset, in winter. She often has a book, maybe it's a prayer book or something and she walks next to the wall of the former abbey."

Of course I immediately thought about the lady I'd seen this afternoon, but that couldn't have been possible. That was just someone mourning at a grave, someone who'd lost a loved one.

Ben proclaimed.

"In the Middle Ages, the plague wreaked havoc on St Andrews. So many people died there was no place to put the corpses. So they put them in a pit, where the Haunted Tower in the cathedral is now. And they sealed the pit with a stone. Years later there were digs there to see if that story was true. They found lots o' coffins and there was the body of a lady wearin' white gloves an' a veil in one o' them."

"And that lady had a disfigured face. They say that she

became a nun to hide her face and never again be seen by others," Donald added.

"In the sixties," Ben continued, getting up, "a student here in St Andrews was walking not too far from the cathedral an' saw a lady dressed in white who waved at him. He walked up to her and then..."

Then Donald got up to mime the scene.

"She took off her veil to show him her face, and he went crazy! Someone found him the next day, lying on one of the graves, repeating: 'The Nun.' He was taken to the insane asylum and never came out again."

After this narrative, the two men sat back down and poured themselves another drink.

"What a tale, huh?"

Here in Scotland people must like to tell ghost stories on Halloween, I thought, before answering them:

"Right. But why does this lady haunt the cemetery?"

"Well, no one ever explained that."

"We've got stories of a White Lady in France too. They say she can be seen next to the road at night when you're driving."

"Aye, but this one is true."

They didn't give me time to refute that. Mathieu came up with his girlfriend.

"Anne, this is Rebecca."

79

I was dazzled by the young lady standing in front of me. Her eyes were surprisingly green, she had long black hair that went down to her hips. Her strange beauty left me speechless. I had no idea where I was nor where I'd been; time stood still as I stared at her, dumbfounded. Rebecca interrupted this spellbound moment, gracefully sitting with us, followed by a "never-thought-this-would-happen-to-me" Mathieu.

"Hi! Here, this is for you."

She handed me a little hollowed-out pumpkin with a candle inside, eyes and a mouth carved out.

"That's to keep the monsters away. I made it for you."

"Thanks, I don't know what to say."

"Don't say anything, just take it."

I was both surprised and a bit uncomfortable. I didn't even know her and she'd brought me something. I suddenly wanted to do anything and everything for her.

"You know, going down to the pier is a good place to pay homage to someone you've lost."

How had she been informed about this? Perhaps she'd seen me? I suddenly felt ridiculous: she must have thought I was crazy, kneeling on the pier with my incense and candles in the wind. I looked at her and couldn't answer. Her penetrating gaze reassured me and brought me into them; I was now slowly rocked by the leaves in the tall trees, and it calmed me down. I trusted her, she knew everything.

"Another good place is the lake. Don't believe what people tell you about it. I often go there to calm down or meditate," she continued.

I wanted to answer her, but I was suddenly exhausted, my head was spinning, my eyelids dropping. Around me objects were distorted, doubled, changing colors. Was I drunk already? I'd only had one glass. The house was full of people I'd never met and I felt as if they were all looking at me. Judging me. In the confusion of laughter mixed with people talking, I heard the words I said, but immediately forgot them. I felt a hand on my hair, but when I turned around, no one was there. Was time out of kilter with me or was it the opposite? Then I was lying on the ground, on my stomach, the cold and damp rock touching my face. What was I doing outside? The wind was still blowing, it was freezing, and it whispered words in my ears that I didn't understand. "*Oidhche Shamhna...*" I got back up, lost in the dark, my footsteps leading me off the beaten path. "*You are the one bringing both worlds together. The one who knows. You picked the four-leaf clover and are protected by our spirits.*"

I found myself at the lakeside. I could make out the silhouette of the house behind me, with glints of light and shadows of party makers moving about. The silence was complete and peculiar. The wind was no longer blowing, branches were no longer moving and even the birds were silent. Only the deep silence of the night. I slow walked up to the lake, its dark and thick waters, and squatted down. I couldn't make out the bottom nor the fish or seaweed below its smooth surface. How deep was it? I had no idea and that made me uncomfortable. This lake was like a huge coffin, a coffin that had attracted Elizabeth's mother and swallowed her up.

"Anne!"

Someone had whispered my name, yet I couldn't see anyone. I got back up.

"Anne!"

It seemed to be coming from the woods right on the side. I slowly walked to them. A few steps later I was beneath the trees, but no one was there.

"Is anyone here?"

No answer. Had I dreamed? Little by little a subdued light broke through: the moon peaked out of the clouds and lit up the landscape. It was as if I had recovered my sight: I was surrounded and protected by huge trees and reflections of the cold light could be seen on the heavy mass of the lake. There was a tree that had fallen in front of me and I sat down on it to admire how calm it was. I felt safe here in the woods. It was so nice to sit here, basking in the night! I closed my eyelids for a few seconds.

Suddenly I heard a soft whisper. I opened my eyes and saw movements on the lakefront. I discreetly walked towards it, hidden behind a tree. It was stemming from several women, who seemed to be disguised, or at least wearing dresses dating back to another era. Each of them had long wavy hair and was wearing a different color: there was ocher, light blue, gray, pink, light green and white. None of them were speaking though their sensual gestures and delicate hands and hair made me think they meant no harm. One of them was touching the water, another was brushing her hair, the one in green was lying on the grass and reading, and the last one was petting a bird perched on her hand. Their movements were all delicately supernatural, yet they appeared familiar to me. I concentrated on their faces: they all had very pale skin, almost translucent, and no expressions at all, only their eyes seemed to be alive. I looked closer: was one of them Rebecca? I was almost sure it was; I recognized her black hair and slightly angular face. I was convinced. It was her.

Then I woke up. The sheets smelled different, they smelled like Mathieu. I turned the light on: this wasn't my room. I was in his bed, completely dressed, and he wasn't there. What was I doing here? I must have gone to bed so drunk that I walked into the wrong room. I got up and returned to my bedroom where I instantaneously fell back asleep.

"The fetus had a heart defect; it couldn't have survived."

"Do you want to organize a funeral? If not, we'll incinerate it and put it in a mass grave."

A mass grave for my baby? White, everything was white and smelled like rubbing alcohol. I felt like I was a part of the mattress, I was so terribly heavy and incapable of moving. White sheets, white walls, midwives in white uniforms.

"Leave me alone. I want to stay with her, read her Pat the Bunny, Dear Zoo, *and* Goodnight Moon."

They looked at each other strangely.

"Ma'am, you don't understand..."

I was so exhausted... Where was my baby? She'd have brown hair like her dad, we'd go to pick blackberries when summer would be drawing to an end. She'd have stains all over her, she wouldn't be able to wait to try them before we made jam.

"Anne, are you okay?"

Guillaume was there, he was pale too. Like the white walls were contagious. I couldn't talk, I wasn't strong enough, my mouth was sealed shut.

"You have to rest my love. We're going back home soon."

She'd have her first bike, her first scooter, her first apartment. She'd grow up, with everyone saying the same thing. *"She looks just like you! The apple doesn't fall far from the tree."* She'd get her first job, have her first child. I'd be a grandma, Guillaume, a grandpa.

I opened my eyes. My nightmare was true. Guillaume was there, holding a little envelope with everything that was left of Lara, a photo and a million dreams of our life with her.

— CHAPTER SIX —

The next morning, I woke up tense and nervous. Dreaming about Lara, again and again—or should I say having nightmares about her—and then, the next day, facing up to the harsh reality of her absence... It was so hard. Despite the months passing, nothing was changing here, I was shattered. Besides, my head was killing me and I barely could remember what I'd done the night before. What day was it? I had no idea. My brain was empty.

I got up and opened the curtains. Outside, the lake lay before me, home to several types of birds.

I went down to the kitchen. William was sitting outside on the porch, having a cup of coffee.

"Mind if I join you?"

"Not at all. Did you sleep well?"

"Not really. I'm exhausted."

"You must have had too much to drink last night."

"Last night?"

Right, the Halloween party. Now I remembered. However, I had no idea what I had done during the party or whom I'd spoken to. I tried to save face.

"Maybe you're right. Did you have a good time?"

"Except that I suddenly found myself all alone! Where'd you go?"

"I don't remember."

"Mathieu took off too, with Rebecca. I had to listen to Ben and Donald's sordid stories all night! Those two never stop!"

"Mathieu's not up yet?"

"He's not back. I think he spent the night at Rebecca's."

"What about Alex?"

"He went to visit his grandma. It's Elizabeth's ninety-fifth birthday."

"Shoot. He promised to tell me when he would see her again. I wish I could talk to her."

"She's sort of senile, you know."

"Maybe, but in some way I feel like I've bonded with her. I sleep in what used to be her room, I know about her life. She's someone I'd really like to meet."

I finished my coffee before it got cold. It was getting overcast and you could see big black clouds rolling in. I shivered. The wind was picking up too and it was getting cooler.

"I stumbled upon a book in the library about all the

Protestant martyrs in St Andrews, especially Patrick Hamilton and George Wishart, and the four others who were burned at the stake."

"Four of them? I thought there were only two others, Henry Forrest and Walter Mill."

"From what the book says, there were six of them in all. I can't remember the names of the other two, but I know that they were sentenced to death before Patrick Hamilton."

"Really? That's interesting. Can you lend it to me? I'd love to leaf through it, that would help me for my dissertation."

"The problem is that I can't find it anymore. I happened upon it when I still worked at the library, but I had to do some photocopies for someone and when I got back, it had disappeared. I thought you may have heard about it, as you've read loads of books on the history of St Andrews."

"True, but not from that time."

"It was an antique leather-bound book. The writing style was old too. At first I thought it was *The History of St Andrews*, but now that Alex lent it to me, I can tell that these are two very different books. I learned lots of interesting stuff, you probably know all of it already. They said that you can make out Patrick Hamilton's face on the facade of the St Salvator Church. Did you know?"

"One of the stones on the tower isn't smooth like the others and its rough edges look like a face. I'll show you next time."

"Thanks."

"You should have stayed with us last night, you would have loved Ben and Donald's tales. They mentioned an urban legend saying that all these martyrs left a mark on St Andrews. Not just the ones who were burned at the stake, but also all those who were tormented and tortured because of what they believed in. Sometimes you see their ghosts, but mostly you hear weird things, like flames burning, people being smothered."

"Oh my god, that's terrible! You wonder where they get all these stories from."

"Lots of sordid stories are told at the university. Not too long ago, a student was said to have fainted at church, because she heard someone screaming and saw faces covered with blood. No one else at church saw or heard a thing."

"She must have been smoking something."

"No need, you know, all these stories make people a little crazy."

Now I was shivering; it was really getting cold. But after all, it was only normal for a month of November. I'd already been here for two months. Time had flown by; I couldn't deny that. William went back to reading his paper.

I decided to leave him and return to my room, where it was nice and warm. The weather sure changed quickly here. I lit up a cigarette and opened the window so the smoke would go out.

The lake was still, calm, and dark. There were swans swimming about, sparrows were flying from tree to tree. All around, I could hear the branches cracking with their minute movements and their leaves blowing around in the wind. So what could I do all day long? It seemed that another idle and boring day was to come... Mathieu wasn't there, meaning I couldn't talk to him about my never-ending nightmare.

I put my cigarette out and went to my desk. There was the four-leaf clover that I'd found when I arrived. I picked it up, observing it curiously. How bizarre! Although I had found it a long time ago, it still was green, as if I had just picked it. It wasn't even dry... Did it bring me luck? I didn't think so, since it hadn't helped me find a good job.

Whatever, anyway, I knew that Guillaume would be there for me if I needed some money, and just this idea demotivated me.

I was tired. In addition to this, I spent all my time thinking about Lara, about all these martyrs who'd perished in St Andrews, about what happened at the lake.

When I glanced at the pumpkin on my table, I suddenly remembered. Rebecca had given it to me the day before. She was so fascinating. And I must have dreamed about her last night. Now I remembered: Rebecca was standing there with several other women, telling me that the lake was a good place... They all had really long hair.

I hadn't gone back to the lake again, and I must admit that now that I knew what had happened there, I was afraid to go. Maybe it was time, though, time to go back to the place I overlooked from my window every morning when getting up and every night, before going to bed. The place that had taken

Elizabeth's mother, linking us together.

I stepped out. A gust of wind blew through my hair as I was going down the little path leading to the lake. Tiny drops of rain hit me directly and my hair turned into minute whisks pounding against my face. The sky was like an immense wound and its black injuries were turning into impressive clouds. I clenched my fists in my pockets and continued walking down the path. Just before arriving, as a precaution, I slowed down a bit.

There it was. Dark water, same color as the sky, with slight ripples on the surface because of the wind. The entire lake was resisting the attack of thousands of raindrops. Vibrating perhaps, but steadfast. I slowly began to walk around it. Its banks seemed to be fragile, ready to fall into the water, so I didn't want to go too close to the edge. I carried on, step by step, mentally measuring how large it was. It wasn't actually that big and in just a few minutes I would have gone around it. It wasn't that frightening either. The color of the water was merely a reflection of the sky. The swans that I'd seen from my window had disappeared, as had the sparrows. I was alone. I continued, carefully, but without any fear. Was the water cool, cold, freezing? I wondered what it would feel like to dive in, would it be thick, would it be light?

I took my shoes off. It felt so good to be barefoot, skin against skin. Its skin was the sweet and damp grass, protecting the access to the lake. I had already gone over halfway around its silhouette. I was holding my shoes in one hand and the other was swaying back and forth, in rhythm with my steps. I put my heel down then my toes, and I felt energy infiltrating me from the ground, running up my leg to my backbone. The lake was robust, beautiful, soft. I knew it well. Each step I took was like a massage that awakened its aching being. I suddenly began to run. My lungs breathed in more air, my lips were smiling tensely, my eyes crying because of the wind, my entire body was wet. I felt like I was alive and I was happy.

I stopped running, out of breath. I had gone around the whole lake. I saw something on the ground and picked it up. It was one of my figurines that I'd bought when I first arrived. A bit farther I saw the other one. What were they doing here? Did someone steal them from my room? Perhaps during the Halloween party? And something even stranger, they actually didn't look like mine. Their posture seemed a bit different, less realistic and gracious. When I'd bought them, they weren't blue, I was pretty sure.

I went into the woods to sit on a tree trunk and rest. I was sheltered from the downpour there. From the inside, the woods looked bigger, like a forest. Despite the many tall trees, it wasn't dark and I could see the sun peeking through their leaves.

How strange it was that the nice weather had suddenly come back! It started to get warm and I was glad of that, as my wet clothing would dry easier. The forest was like a microcosm. Everything was so beautiful here: the moist mushrooms I could smell, the way the trees moved, the sunbeams, life wherever you looked, a myriad of birds, insects, and spiders. And in the background, the urban hustle and bustle, the ordinary lives of human beings in the town. I loved nature so much that I could have cried, just thinking of it. Perfection. We also were a part of this perfection, so minute and insignificant compared to nature as a whole. In this peculiar state of mind, I remained seated in the middle of the forest, looking at the clouds and the insects and plants. I had no idea why. It seemed to me that their colors could make me cry from emotion. I physically felt weak though strong inside.

I began to speak. I couldn't stop speaking, describing the scenery to her. I was holding Lara's hand, because she was afraid when she was in the woods. We had arrived at the fence at the end of the woods, I started to climb over it.

She seemed anxious.

"Mommy, where are we going?"

"Don't worry sweetie, we won't get lost."

We continued, our feet getting stuck in the mud, tripping because it was now dark out. Both of us ran, laughing like little kids. We followed a narrow path and suddenly arrived at a huge flat field, right at the top, with the land on one side and the sea on the other, as far as the eye could see. We both were happy, alone amidst nature. I filled my eyes with this beautiful landscape. The sky was immense and there were thousands of twinkling stars. We both danced in the middle of the field, twirling around and it was magnificent wherever we looked.

Then we went back down. It was dark so we couldn't see much but we knew that we'd have to be careful to the huge lumps of earth and troughs, as the field had been plowed. In the night our eyes got bigger so we saw better. Some thistles stuck on my legs. I showed Lara how to appreciate all of this, the beauty of simple things, the freedom each person has to make the most of their lives, to enjoy nice things. She was afraid of the dark, she was cold and the thistles were pricking her, but I was there to protect her. I liked the dark night and adventure, I was no longer cold, I didn't blame the elements. It was windy, but that was a part of the beauty; the thistles weren't pricking me, I was the one who was walking on them and hurting myself.

She looked at me.

"Am I dreaming mommy?"

"Honey, unfortunately, I think so... We're beyond the limits of time. Come on, we're almost home."

We were nearing the door and we both had lots of thistles stuck on our clothes.

She tried to take them off.

"Mommy, I can't get rid of them!"

I reassured her.

"Just leave them sweetie. They're the proof that this wasn't a dream, that it really happened. Life is just as beautiful as that."

She suddenly disappeared; I was no longer holding her hand.

"Lara?"

I turned around, but she was no longer there. The wind was gusting and now I was freezing. It was dark out and there were no street lights, I was all alone. I looked at my coat: there were thistle blossoms on it. What had really happened in the woods?

Slowly coming back to reality, I went in. There was a red ribbon on the doorknob. Left over from the party? Without even trying to see if the guys were at home, I walked up to my room, still shaken by what I had just experienced. What was happening to me? I had gone out at the beginning of the afternoon and now night had already fallen! My clothes were dirty, I was barefoot, my coat was full of grass and thistles. I slowly got undressed. Were all these things that I'd seen true? My heart hoped so, but my brain told me the opposite: Lara couldn't be... I suddenly doubted. Maybe they'd lied to me? After all, did I really know what had happened at the hospital? They'd given me so much medication that I could no longer think clearly, I would have believed anything they'd told me. Perhaps they'd stolen Lara, perhaps she was still alive. I was happy just thinking of this. But I suddenly realized that it wasn't plausible. Lara would have just been one year old. She wouldn't have been able to walk, talk, or even be here, lost in the middle of Scotland. What had happened was just a dream then. Perhaps I'd dozed off, it was so nice and warm in the woods. Yes, but all those thistles on my coat? They were real, I could feel them, I had to pull hard so they'd come out of my coat, they pricked my fingers.

I went into the bathroom and turned on the faucets in the tub. I looked at my reflection in the mirror. What was happening to me? I felt like I was going crazy. Nothing was making sense anymore here. All those objects moving around, all those sleepless nights. I was afraid. The bathroom was steaming up, like fog surrounding me and making me disappear.

Lara's funeral. Getting dressed up to see my dead baby was unnatural. Putting on makeup while crying was impossible... I remembered her little white coffin.

I put one foot into the tub, then the other, and lay down. When all was said and done, leaving France hadn't helped me. I was useless, I couldn't find myself a decent job and was still mourning my daughter. I wasn't progressing, my life was stagnating. I was like dirty, foul water.

I tried to turn the faucets on. Once again, they were blocked and even by forcing them, they wouldn't budge. I didn't know why, perhaps they were rusty or maybe all the limestone prevented them from turning. They looked so old. I tried several times, I wanted to call someone, but gave up. I couldn't stop the water from running. I didn't care. My life was worth nothing. I put my head under the water, letting the water into my ears and nostrils, letting my hair float. I had intentionally gone into the lake to know what it felt like to have been penetrated by its stagnant water. We were both the same after all: we couldn't change our nature. Neither of us would ever progress. I wanted to become a part of it, I wanted its water to purify me and take me away forever. I could hear my heart beating slower and slower. I'd finally join Lara. Join Elizabeth's mother too. That was how it should be as I was incapable of giving life. I'd be free from what was weighing me down.

I suddenly felt a hand pulling my head out of the water. The same hands turned the faucets off and stopped the hemorrhage of the bathwater.

"Anne, what the hell are you doing? There's water in the hall!"

It was Mathieu. I could hear Alex too.

"The carpet is soaked! It'll take days to dry out!"

Mathieu handed me a towel and emptied the bathtub by taking the stopper out. I looked at him silently: I felt as calm as I had been in the forest, as peaceful as if I'd slept all night. He energetically dried me off with the towel, then put both hands on my shoulders and looked at me.

"You know you're like a sister to me, right? I don't want anything to happen to you."

— CHAPTER SEVEN —

After that I slept for twenty-four hours straight. When I finally woke up, I felt like I had been stabbed in the heart. I remembered exactly what had occurred, even though I found it hard to admit it. Mathieu must have told them everything as he was the one who found me in the bathroom and he knew what I had done. I was ashamed of myself and wished none of this was real. I couldn't just get up as if nothing had happened and say hi to everyone. So I remained lying, just waiting. When I finally would go out of my bed, perhaps my friends would have forgotten all of this.

I heard the door open and someone walking up to the bed but I kept my eyelids closed and pretended to still be asleep. I didn't want to see anyone, I just wanted them to leave me alone. What must they be thinking of me! The only friends I had... As they had become true friends now, me, since I was no longer in touch with any of my former ones. They had accepted me as I was. I felt like they listened to me, that they even appreciated me. The sound of the footsteps faded away. I waited for a while without moving, then opened my eyes. They had brought me a carafe of water and a glass: I immediately poured myself something to drink. A bouquet of flowers had been placed on the desk.

I got up to pick up the picture inside my wardrobe door, then returned to bed.

No, I didn't forget you Lara. I think of you every day and I'll remember you as long as I live. I lost you, but that was our fate. Now I have to learn to live without you. You have to leave me.

I put the photo under my pillow. I had to fight. To be strong. For me, but for my friends too, and for Guillaume, for my parents. I remembered the good times we had had together. Down south, in our sun-kissed village, in our warm house. Memories from these good old days went through my head: the smell of spices in the kitchen, the fragrance of thyme, the sun on the patio, the chirping of the crickets. An abundance of light and flowers. The hot summer weather slowly warming me. I'd left this place where I was born, eager to escape. I'd abandoned my family to live here, in this unknown, damp and gray country. I'd be going back in just another month. I'd be returning *home* and could finally hug Guillaume.

I dozed off again for a few hours. When I woke up, it was all dark. Everything was calm in the house, and so was I finally. I lit a cigarette and sat on the windowsill, looking out. The clouds were hiding the stars away from me but I could see the moon, and admired it peacefully while I smoked. Every once in a while, I could hear a night owl hooting. A cool breeze came in and woke me up completely this time. I was famished. I finished my cigarette and went down to the kitchen.

This was the first time I'd been out of my room since the incident—little by little, I got back in touch with the house. Unfortunately for me, the fridge was nearly empty: a few beers, some milk, a bit of cheddar, eggs, and a few yogurts. I drank the milk straight from the bottle, then opened the cupboards to find something to nibble on: a leftover sponge cake would have to do.

Then I headed upstairs. The bathroom was right in front of me. I hesitated to open the door, just to see, but it was still much too recent so I turned around and took refuge in my bedroom.

It was only the next morning that I felt ready to face everyone. I dragged myself downstairs. Mathieu was the first one to see me and immediately walked up to me.

"Anne, finally! You have no idea how worried we were! Are you feeling better?"

I nodded, with a timid smile. Alex waved at me.

"Hi Anne."

"You need to have your breakfast, you haven't eaten for days," Mathieu exclaimed, bringing me a heaping plate of pancakes, scrambled eggs and bacon.

"Your favorite breakfast!"

William walked in and patted me on the shoulder.

"And we've even got..."

And he put a bag of French pastry on the table. My mouth dropped open.

"Croissants! Where did you find them?"

"It looks like we know how to make you talk again! Just need a bag of fresh French croissants from the bakery!"

I flashed a smile. I hadn't had these for ages! They were delicious, crispy and buttery. I felt like I was surfing on a wave of happiness. This was where I belonged, with people I liked, enjoying the beautiful Scottish scenery. I looked at them, listened to them, without speaking.

"Thank you, guys. You are the best."

"We want you to get well soon. Tonight we're going to the pub. In the meanwhile, I have to work on my dissertation."

A croissant in one hand and a forkful of bacon in the other, I waved at William as he left.

Alex handed me an airmail letter.

"You've got mail."

This letter came from afar. From France. I thanked him and put it aside so I could read it when I was alone. Mathieu seemed to have something on his mind.

"Anne, we have to talk about what happened. I know you just got up, but I'm worried about you."

He paused. Alex discreetly left.

"I want to be sure that you're alright and that this won't

happen again. Was... Was there something in your room that made you do that? You have to tell me."

"No, it wasn't in my room."

"Not in your room? Where then?"

"At the lake. I went down to the lake."

"Why did you go there? After everything that happened there! You know it's dangerous."

"Yeah, but Rebecca said that she often walk around there. I just wanted to see..."

"See what? Rebecca never goes near water, she's afraid of it. You must have misunderstood."

"Mathieu, I saw Lara at the lake. I think I'm having hallucinations. That's why..."

The words froze on my lips and I was unable to finish my sentence. I still couldn't admit what I'd done. Mathieu looked at me anxiously.

"Anne, you have to overcome your sadness. I know that this seems hard, but it's not impossible. If not, you're going to go crazy."

"I know."

"Find something to do. Look for a job, read some books. You seemed interested by the history of the town. Did you find *The History of St Andrews*?"

"Alex lent it to me," I nodded.

"Perfect. You'll sleep in my room for a while. That way you won't have the view that overlooks the lake."

"But... No, I want to stay in Elizabeth's room!"

"Anne, it's for your own good. You can go back later, when you're feeling better. In the meanwhile, I'll move into your room. You mean too much to me for me to lose you."

Upon hearing this I couldn't help myself; all the emotions of the past few days submerged me and I broke down in tears. Mathieu hugged me until I calmed down.

"Crying does you good. After that, you'll take a nice hot shower in the downstairs bathroom. Then you'll bring your stuff into my room and we'll head into town. Feeling better?"

I grabbed the letter and returned to my room to read it. I immediately recognized my mom's beautiful handwriting, and with a twinge of sorrow I opened the envelope.

There was only one short paragraph.

"Anne,

You left because you were hopeless. Here not a day goes by without us thinking of you, talking about you, looking at photos of you. Time passes, but we still don't have any news. How are you feeling? When are you coming back? We can't wait until you come back home again. And we want you to know that we love you more than anything.

Mom"

And on the bottom:

"Come back! Dad."

These words had two meanings; it touched me. My parents asked me not only to come back from Scotland, but to forgive them and go see them. Last time things didn't go well at all. I hadn't really decided not to see them after that, but that's how things just went. At that time, little by little I had refused to see people again and I remained inside so I wouldn't stumble upon someone I knew. I suddenly felt nostalgic. I knew I had been harsh with them and that I made them unhappy when I'd left. I realized how selfish I had been, acting blindly out of grief.

There was also a letter from my fiancé. Guillaume. I hadn't given him any news for a while. He didn't even have my phone number. I had wanted to leave everyone that I knew, become someone else and start my new life here, in St Andrews. What I hadn't realized, though, is that meant that I'd also have to forget what was the most important to my eyes: my family.

I opened his letter, with shaking hands. As I read it, I could almost hear Guillaume whispering these words in my ear:

"Darling,

I'm using your parents' letter here to join one too. This is the first time I've actually written a real letter to you, if we forget that disastrous declaration of love when we were both students. Well, maybe it wasn't that disastrous, as you said 'Yes' when I asked you to marry me!

The house seems too big without you. When we bought it together two years ago, I never thought I'd be living in it alone one day. The garden is full of weeds without you and the living room needs your expert hands and ideas in decoration.

I ran across your colleague Clarisse, a few days ago: she said that the girl who's replacing you is a real bitch and everyone misses you.

Anne, I'd really like some sort of sign from you. Something that proves that you haven't forgotten me. I do understand that you want to start over again, your impression that you've got nothing to lose now. But in reality, you've still got a lot to lose: a loyal fiancé, parents who love you, and your life here. Please, I'm begging you, don't forget everything, don't forget us. Some things are worth remembering. Memories, both good and bad, forge our identity. All the trials and pain that life puts in our paths make us stronger.

If you come back, I promise that things will be better. I've probably been awkward, but that was the way I coped with our baby's passing. That was my way of being a man: a man doesn't show his feelings. I thought that if I did that, everything would be easier for you.

Don't forget your promise when I kneeled down at the restaurant to ask you to marry me. Don't forget that you said 'Yes' before hugging and kissing me after.

We've still got so much to experience. The wedding is just waiting for you to come back to take place. Life is holding its arms out to us, but for that, we have to be together. For that, you have to come back.

Make the right decision. I love you.

Guillaume."

My heart was broken when I read his words. Yes, I had made a promise to him. I picked up my phone, ready to call him.

But I immediately put it back down. What could I tell him? Of course, I still had feelings for him and loved him, but I couldn't say that I suffered being far from him. My broken heart had closed up like an oyster, to protect itself. Guillaume... I had started to forget the details of his face. Yes, he was a part of my life before. But I'd gotten used to living without him, living far from my loved ones. They no longer were a part of my present. It was *my* universe, *my* new life. I didn't want his voice to rekindle memories of the past, rekindle my love for him. Not yet. For now, I just wanted to concentrate on my Scottish journey.

I looked at my calendar: December 20th was circled. I still hadn't let Guillaume know that I'd booked the flight. I had a bit more than a month to finish what I'd come here for. And after that, I'd made up my mind, I'd go back to my former life in France.

I spent the afternoon with Mathieu and William in a cute little cafe in the town center, one I'd not yet been to in the two months I'd been here. Sipping on piping hot chocolate with whipped cream and slivered chocolate, in a cozy atmosphere, we talked about our childhood. All these memories that we shared made me even more melancholic than the letters I had just read. My friends understood my feelings too: all three of us were expats and none of us had seen our families for a while, making our souvenirs even more sensitive and filled with emotion. You could say that all three of us had left our roots to be able to talk about them even better: I had never felt so French since I'd been living abroad.

I watched them attentively, Mathieu with his pale skin and little black glasses, and William looking like an American actor from the sixties. I wondered where they'd both be in ten years. And where would I be? I had no idea.

In the evening, Alex joined us at The Drinking Bastards Pub. It was packed. We made our way through the crowd in front of the bar, our shoes making sticking on the dirty floor. Two heavy Scottish drinkers with rosy cheeks were leaning on the bar counter, laughing and sputtering loudly. We finally found a table at the back.

I raised my glass of beer.

"Here's to you my friends and thank you again for everything."

They just shrugged.

"Cheers!"

And we all started on our drinks. William had a white mustache on his lips, making us all laugh. I felt good with them.

I hadn't been alone for a single minute the whole afternoon so I didn't have time for any dark thoughts. I knew that they weren't buried very deeply, though.

"Alex, by the way, did you see Elizabeth?"

"Yup, it was her birthday."

"You said you'd introduce her to me."

"You're right. But I don't think you're ready yet. Next time."

I didn't insist. He must be right. But I really did want to meet her before leaving.

The atmosphere in the pub was picking up pace: there was an improvised contest of who could drink the most glasses of Guinness.

"Those guys are crazy," Mathieu observed. "After just one pint of Guinness, my stomach feels like a basketball! No way could I ever drink several pints!"

"A Guinness is a whole meal, you've got something to eat and drink," added William.

I'd never tried one. Our mouths hung open as we watched them empty huge glasses of beer in one single swallow. A relentless mechanism! The glasses were filled, then huge arms raised them; most of the content was gulped down, with drops of beer running down long black or gray beards; then the empty glass was placed on the counter, as if a battle had been won. Sometimes a loud burp could be heard before starting the cycle once again. Anyway, the contest came to an end with shouts and applause for the winner who had greedily drunk eleven pints of Guinness in less than ten minutes, nearly a gallon and a half of beer.

I took advantage of the relative calm at the bar to get refills for my friends. The owner was running all over.

"Is it okay if I use your glasses again? I don't have any clean glasses. Our girl left and I'm a bit overwhelmed here."

I suddenly remembered that the last time I'd come here, he was looking for someone to hire as his waitress was pregnant and would soon be leaving.

"You didn't find anyone?"

"No! No one was breaking the door down to work here. People prefer to come to drink rather than to pour drinks. Same thing?"

"Yeah, three Gordons and one Guinness please."

I started thinking while he filled the glasses up. I was available. Maybe this position would help me bounce back. It would only be for a while, I'd earn a little bit of money and meet new people. Even though this wasn't a dream job for me it would be better than staying home and having hallucinations.

I decided to try my luck, after all, I had picked up a four-leaf clover!

"Would you hire a French person? I'm looking for a job. And I've got a Scottish social security number."

"Well, if you can keep that nice smile on your face and you're not afraid of big drinkers, you can start tomorrow! But this is no pleasure trip, I have to warn you."

"Good. I don't like standing around doing nothing. I can come tomorrow then?"

"Sure, around eleven then. I'll show you the ropes here."

"Thanks a lot!"

And I went back with full glasses and a heart filled with joy. No need to spend hours at the Job Center when you could just talk to a barman!

"Guess what? I just got myself a JOB!"

My three friends looked at me, amazed, and listened to my little story. Mathieu was a bit skeptical: that wasn't the kind of job he saw me doing, I could have found something better... But finally he ended up agreeing with me that it would get my mind off things and all four of us raised a toast to my new future.

Alex looked at my glass.

"You ordered a Guinness? Too good for our local Edinburgh Gordons?

"I wanted to try it, I've never had any before."

"Never? Watch out, you're drinking enemy beer here! Guinness is Irish, even if lots of Scots drink it."

I looked down at this famous beverage I was holding in my hand, a blackish liquid covered with beige foam, then put my lips to the glass. It was a refreshing and a bit sparkling beer, with a slight note of coffee and a hint of bitterness.

"So?"

"Not bad. Different. A little bitter."

Mathieu pointed something out to me.

"And you'll notice that it's not black, but dark red. I lost five bucks on a bet about that."

I lifted my glass to look, and he was right. The beer was actually a dark shade of Bordeaux. We all laughed. I was happy, I was with my friends.

We finally headed back home. On the way, we came across police officers who were ticketing people who were either drunk or drinking on public roads. They didn't mess with the rules in the United Kingdom!

The door wasn't locked, as usual. That always surprised me, anyone could just turn the doorknob and walk in. I never would have done that in France. But here people respected private property.

It was my first night in Mathieu's room. He'd removed his clothes and taken up residence in the room overlooking the lake. I actually was sleeping just a few yards from my "old" bedroom, as Mathieu's was just on the other side of the bathroom, on the same floor. Now I understood why he was the first one to have found me in the bathroom the day ... was it just the day before? No, it wasn't because I had slept for a long time. Was it two, or three days ago then? I'd lost the notion of time; I had the impression that it had happened ages ago. I even felt that it hadn't happened to me, but to someone else, or perhaps *I* was someone else then, someone far from reality.

His room was a typical male one. I had to force myself not to pick up after him. Mathieu wouldn't like it if I moved his stuff. Maybe I could clean a little someday. I put some of my clothes on an empty shelf and looked around. There was a copy of Van Gogh's sunflowers, signed "*Vincent*," on the wall. His window overlooked the road and I chuckled to myself when I saw that it also overlooked Rebecca's room. I imagined Mathieu sitting there for hours on end, gazing at her.

There was a lot of corrected homework on his desk, and a bouquet of blue thistles. You could find them all over in the countryside here. He had an alarm clock on his bedside table, a small scale and a bell too. I wondered why, were they decorations or maybe souvenirs from his family? Or perhaps he used them, but for what? I had no idea. It might not have been good manners to ask all these questions, after all, he was lending his room to me and I shouldn't have been poring over everything in it. I couldn't help myself, though, I was curious.

I walked up to the bookshelves and looked at his books. Of course he had a huge French-English dictionary, grammar and conjugation books, and ones on French history. I wondered what kind of teacher Mathieu was: one that his students loved? Did they participate or did he just give lectures? Did his students nickname him "The Frog[1]"? I smiled. I glanced at the other books: the history of golf in St Andrews, a biography of Mozart, a five-volume encyclopedia, and then I jumped, surprised. After a second of hesitation, I delicately pulled the book out. This was it. The book I'd seen in the library. The old book I'd been looking for ages, the one with the cover that had seen better days. It was heavy. Written on old and thick paper. I immediately regretted not having asked Mathieu about it as he would have simply told me that he had the book in his room. He must have borrowed it from the library, yet it wasn't labeled with the Dewey Decimal Classification at all. Had he stolen it before it was processed? Was it a different book? Impossible, it was the one I'd held in my hands.

Though it was late, I sat down and this time, really read it through. It wouldn't escape me again. I opened it up, making the cover crack and releasing a smell of old paper. I could see the stitching, the thread holding the pages together and binding them to the leather cover. I looked at the first page. The title said, in capital letters:

THE CITY OF ST ANDREWS

On the bottom, I read that it had been published in Edinburgh, by Dakin & Co, Castle Street, in 1849.

---

[1] "Frogs" is a slang term used by the English since the eighteenth century to talk about the French, perhaps as they are known for eating frog legs.

A book about St Andrews, I hadn't imagined it. There was a two-page lithography of the town. You could see all the monuments: the cathedral, the castle, a church, with peasants in the foreground and a ship sailing on the sea in the background. I delicately turned the page.

The text began, in Old English. It started off on the legend of how Regulus had founded the city, just as William had told me. The monk had brought relics of Saint Andrew in his boat here after having had a vision. Then there was another part on religion, as St Andrews was formerly an ecclesiastical hub. I skipped the pages on the famous bishops and archbishops who had lived here. There was also a section on the university, its professors and its students. Then I reached the part about the martyrs. I read it again. There were five martyrs who had perished here in St Andrews, and one in Perth.

I remembered the urban legend William had told me about—the one that said that ghosts of people who had suffered, like these poor martyrs, had left their mark on some places in town. That girl had heard screaming in a church and had fainted. Ghosts had taken possession of some places... And I hadn't felt too well either in Saint Trinity Church during Mathieu's organ concert: the impression I had that everyone was looking at me, the frightening shadows made by the candles, the death rattle I thought I'd heard. I leafed through the book until I found something that interested me.

"In 1586, St Andrews was infested by the plague, killing four thousand people and leaving the town nearly deserted. The epidemic had started on one side of the town, but no one remained

quarantined at home, so it rapidly spread all over. Some people believed that breathing in smells of tar, sulfur or petrol would save them. Others decided to shelter themselves in boats, the richest people on large ships, fishermen in their own boats, but most were in such a hurry that they forgot to take food and water, and also perished. Several boats drifted for days before someone could take care of the dead bodies. People were ruthless: children left their parents, some parents abandoned their children to protect themselves, others assassinated them so they wouldn't suffer, women died giving birth alone. Each night, dead bodies were removed from churches and their clothing was burned before burying them. The town was completely silent. Those who had escaped death from the plague wandered around town, not knowing where to go, and often died by starvation.

All of Scotland was panicked. In 1597, St Andrews was a victim of the plague, famine, and witch hunts. People were afraid of dying without having received the last sacraments. They believed that the plague only attacked sinners. This climate led to a generalized suspicion and as blame had to be given to someone, witches were accused and burned to try to eradicate this evil and solicit God's favors."

What an awful era! The plague and witch hunts in this little town. There was nothing about the Abbey wall or the Haunted Tower being a mass grave. Maybe Ben and Donald had made that up.

I started to yawn and looked at my watch: 3 a.m. Time for bed. I put my pajamas on and lay down: I wished good night to Lara's photo and put my hands under the pillow to put it away

114

when my fingers touched a cold object. There was something under.

I sat up and picked the pillow up to see what it was—a knife. I couldn't believe my eyes. A knife? What was Mathieu doing with this under his pillow? Was he afraid of being attacked? Then I heard a strange creaking noise that scared me half to death. I saw a shadow. I picked up the knife and turned around: nothing. I had to go see Mathieu, even if I had to wake him up. He had to explain what this was about. My heart pounding, holding the knife in my hand, I stepped out. I delicately put one foot in front of the other, without making a sound. Just a few steps and I was standing in front of my room—Elizabeth's room, the one Mathieu was in now. I gently rapped on the door. No answer. I knocked again. He must be sound asleep. I wanted to check and I opened the door, allowing myself to enter. For a second I thought I saw shadowy forms dancing on the wall, about ten of them. Then they stopped. It must have been the trees outside. I walked to the bed; it was empty. No Mathieu. I was suddenly afraid. Where was he? The blade was shining brightly in my hand, a reflection of the moon.

"Anne?"

Someone had whispered my name behind me. My hand was shaking. I tightened my grip on the handle of the knife and turned around.

"What are you doing, Anne?"

It was William. He'd heard me knocking on the door and it woke him up.

"And what's with that knife? Give it to me."

I could see by the look in his eyes that he was worried. I relaxed and let him take the knife.

"Sorry."

"You should go back to bed. You're sleeping in Mathieu's room tonight. What happened? Did you see something?"

"I was looking for Mathieu. He's not here..."

"Well, you shouldn't be walking around with sharp objects. That's dangerous."

"I know, but..."

"I'm going to put this knife back in the kitchen where it belongs. And don't you go get it again. It's safe here."

I didn't answer. He waited for me to go out before leaving. I could feel his gaze following me until I returned to Mathieu's room.

"Night."

"Night."

I opened the door and turned on the light. They'd told me dozens of times not to lock my door, but this time I was afraid and did it anyway. The lock made a muffled click upon closing. Then, silence. I already felt better. Maybe I'd finally get some rest. At the end of the day, all these stories about locks and keys were just old wives' tales. When I walked to the bed and mechanically looked out the window, my heart almost stopped. Rebecca was staring at me, both shoulders facing the pane, her black hair falling straight like two waterfalls on each side of her face. She was completely immobile and didn't greet me. Her penetrating glaze went right through me. Was she astonished that I was in Mathieu's room? She kept staring right at me, standing motionless.

I suddenly heard a loud slam, like a chain reaction, louder and louder. I had to cover my ears with my hands. The window blew open and almost hit me right in the face, the door was being shaken on its hinges, and a gust of wind seemed to blow through the room, causing the window to open and slam shut again and again. I went to the door, struggling against the wind blowing in my ears, with a deafening racket. I heard someone shouting out my name from the other side of the door.

"Anne! Anne! Can you hear me? It's Alex!"

"I hear you!"

"Un..."

"What?"

The wind had swallowed his words. Both doors and windows were slamming, it seemed to me that the entire house was trembling in an immense cacophony.

"Anne o..."

It was like the door was going to be blown away. Like it had been driven from the inside, had gone crazy. Muffled noises were hammering in my head: it was as if someone was banging on the wall with a mace.

"Anne, open the do…"

I suddenly understood. He wanted me to unlock the door. At the very instant I turned the key, everything stopped: the wind ceased, there was no more sound and the windows stopped slamming shut. I opened the door and looked at Alex. William was just behind him, on the landing.

"Anne, we told you never to lock your door!"

"I know, but I got scared tonight."

"Why, what got into you? You should have felt better in this room."

"Yeah, I know, but… I told you, I was scared."

"It'll be worse if you don't listen to us. Look what happened! Elizabeth was clear about this and I respect her: you never lock any doors here."

"What were all these doors and windows slamming shut then? A message from beyond?"

Though I'd asked this question with a slight laugh, deep down inside, I was starting to wonder. Alex didn't answer right away.

"You know that stuff took place here. This house witnessed moments of tragedy as well as happiness. It's extremely old. It's normal that it has some presences in it."

He stopped for a second, and then went on:

"If those presences bother you, you'll have to find another place to live in. We already talked about this. Or else, you just accept them, and above all, respect them. Understand? It's up to you."

So it was true then, we were living in a haunted house. When he'd explained to me that some people had heard noises and left, he knew. This was no urban legend. Yet, at the beginning he let me believe that some of these stories weren't really true. That must be Lochan Wynd's real secret, not just Elizabeth's story.

Alex broke off my train of thought.

"Why don't we all go to bed? We'll talk about this tomorrow. Sleep on it."

Everyone went back into their respective rooms. I walked up to the window. In the dark Lochan Wynd road, all the houses seemed to be sleeping. At Rebecca's, the curtains were closed and lights off.

What role had Rebecca played in what had just happened? I couldn't figure her attitude out; why had she stared at me like that? She was why I'd gone down to the lake. Where was Mathieu and why had he left me a knife under the pillow? I didn't understand.

I lay down and continued thinking, eyes wide open in my dark room. I was being taunted by a sleep I knew I'd never reach tonight. The air slowly filled itself with sounds and light. Where was I? I saw shadows flitting around although no one was here.

The bed finally swallowed me up in the ocean of night.

— CHAPTER EIGHT —

Morning finally came and I hadn't really closed my eyes for the whole night. I didn't want to see Alex and have him ask me what decision I had made. I had had enough time to think things over and I had decided not to leave. In just over a month, I'd be flying back to France, and no way was I going to move again for just a few weeks. I'd promise my friends I wouldn't do anything stupid.

When I finally got up, the house was empty: they all must have gone to class. Around eleven, I went to The Drinking Bastards. I was enthusiastic when I opened the door and saw the owner.

"Here you are then. I must admit, I didn't think you'd show. Promises given around a glass of beer are quickly forgotten."

"I'm not a liar!"

"I'm Adam," he said, offering me his hand.

I shook it and answered:

"Anne."

"Nice to meet you."

Adam showed me around the pub: the counter, the main room, the restrooms, the storage area and the kitchen. At noon he also had a brasserie restaurant service. My tasks would be to help him with the bar, to wait on tables at noon and clear them, to clean the restrooms, the pub area and do the dishes. Tuesday to Saturday. Not really my cup of tea but that would do. I signed the contract. I was thrilled.

For my first day at the pub, I shadowed Adam and tried to remember as much as I could. I took orders and gave them to him. I was a little stressed-out as I was doing this in a foreign language; besides I'd never worked in a restaurant before. But things were different here.

At noon, a few people ordered meals: fries, pizzas, fish pies. I informed the cook and waited on the tables: just one dish at a time to begin with. Then I had to clear the tables and do the washing-up. That was my true introduction to catering and restaurant services. I had to sort the plates, put the cutlery together in little baskets, the plates and glasses in another one and then put everything in a huge steam driven dishwasher. Waste had to be sorted too with plastic in the bin and leftover food in the garbage disposal. I'd never used one before, it was like a huge stomach, digesting everything it swallowed. Mankind bought, consumed, and wasted. All this uneaten food reminded me of the ruin of civilization. In this universe of decay, I, wearing a hairnet and gloves, felt like I was a surgeon trying to save people.

I was happy that I was finally useful to someone. It was a job where I was on my feet all the time, making me sweat and move around. Things got quiet after lunch and I finally had enough time to clean the tables properly, to dry the dishes and to put them away.

Adam showed me how to pour a Guinness properly.

"It's actually quite an art and customers could refuse it if it wasn't prepared correctly. You have to hold your glass at a 45-degree angle. You begin to fill it until it's three-quarters full, then you wait for the Guinness to settle and the foam to thin for two minutes. After that, you continue to fill the glass until the dome-shaped head is formed. The foam—a creamy hat—has to be nice and thick."

Then he smiled and showed me the sign right in front of the Guinness tap.

"Then you serve it, and make sure that your customer is respecting the *Six Steps to Drink Guinness!*"

And there actually were six points on the sign.

"*1. Admire the beauty of your glass of Guinness, raising it up to your eyes.*

2. Control your glass of Guinness and be proud of yourself: 'This is my pint. I deserve it.'

3. Raise your elbow.

4. Tilt your glass at the same time as your head to drink it.

5. Always drink on the same side of your glass: you'll have

parallel lines on your glass, each time you take a sip. A proper
Guinness drinker should leave nine rings on his glass, meaning
he'll have taken nine sips to finish it.

  6. Drink reasonably."

I smiled as I read it.

"Lots of people around here don't drink Guinness, they prefer Gordon," continued Adam. "It's not a bad beer either and you also have to respect it when serving it. People drink a lot of sherry and whisky around here too. So for the whisky, we've got a few very good bottles in stock that we reserve for our most demanding customers. Here they try it, before ordering a glass. And we serve them a glass of water at the same time so that they can quench their thirst while enjoying the aroma of their whisky. Chardonnay wine is also a good seller here for the ladies, but I guess that you know how to serve a glass of wine."

I nodded.

"Here it's considered classy to drink Chardonnay," he said. "Oh, I forgot something. We usually don't drink with our customers. But sometimes we have to, you'll see. So, it's up to you, but make sure you remain sober so you can keep working."

"Sure. That won't be a problem for me!"

"I'll close up, but sometimes you might have to work late. But your regular hours will be from 11 to 2 and 5 to 10 p.m."

"Okay."

"I think we've covered everything here. You can go now if

you want. For a first day, you did a good job. So tomorrow you can start with your normal schedule."

I thanked him and left, humming, wandering down St Andrews' cobbled streets in this cold and gray day. I felt like wandering around before going back home and walked to St Salvator's Chapel. The PH slab at my feet was still there. I made sure I didn't step on it and raised my head to look at the stones on the clock tower. Looking up, into the sun, blinded me, and for a fleeting moment I thought I'd fall. I saw black stars floating in my eyes. I lowered my head to collect my wits before slowly raising it again, to look at that infamous stone.

There it was: I could make out two sunken eyes on the facade with a large forehead and a round mouth. The spitting image of Patrick Hamilton's face. Or should I have said his face distorted by pain, with bulging eyes and swollen cheeks. I suddenly wanted to observe each place where those poor martyrs had perished, to see if there was something left.

George Wishart, in front of the castle. I quickly walked there. I went up North Street and took the first road on the left, North Castle Street. This was a simply charming little road: stone houses with white painted windows, ivy climbing up their facades, flowerpots on their moss-covered steps, with a view of the castle and the sea in the background. In just a few minutes, I'd reached the GW initials remaining on the pavement just outside the ruins of the St Andrew's Castle.

How could I be sure that this was precisely where he'd perished? I could see the slab right in front of me in the tar road, less than three feet from the sidewalk. Back in the day the road must have been some sort of unpaved median. I was sure that the fence surrounding the castle didn't exist at that time. I didn't think the slab dated back either, or perhaps it had been rebuilt: all the cobblestones seemed to be new.

I wondered if the other martyrs had slabs too. What were their names again? I had read that in the book last night. There were four of them listed on Martyr's Monument, Hamilton, Wishart and ... and Forrest and Myln! Nailed it! *"Henry Forrest was burned at the stake in front of the northern door of the cathedral."* That was right next to the castle, I headed there immediately.

Going down the narrow East Scores Road from the hilltop, you overlooked the sea on your left and the cemetery and ruins of St Andrews Cathedral on your right. It was calm and I could only hear the wind and the waves breaking on the rocks. The sky was getting darker, full of gray clouds that were reflected in the sea, a subtle tone-on-tone picture. The road narrowed, turning into a mere path. I reached the cathedral's outer wall. The northern door... Where could that be now? I seriously lacked any sense of direction and had no idea which way was north. I decided to go around the outer wall. There was a small door leading to the cemetery and the ruins of the cathedral, but it seemed much too simple to be that "northern gate" I was looking for.

I continued. Seagulls were perched on top of the wall, facing the sea, and I felt like they were watching me and making fun of me. I reached an old tower with a little mound full of grass and abandoned stones. There was a little sign saying that St Mary on the Rocks Church was formerly there. From there I could see the stone pier that I loved walking on and the port. I went towards the right to continue going around the ramparts. It was quite long actually. There were towers here and there. A bit beyond the port, there was an arch announcing the beginning of Pends Road. I took this road on the right, still following the stone walls.

A few minutes later I reached a gate leading to the cemetery and the ruins of the cloister and priory. I looked on the ground but didn't see any commemorative slab. Then I walked under a double arch, before arriving to the top of South Street.

The main entrance of the cathedral, now in ruins, was on the city side. I'd gone around the square fortifications without discovering any trace of that poor martyr, Forrest. I'd need more information to find out where it took place. Or perhaps traces of what happened in the past were now below the tar, out of my reach.

Then there was Walter Myln, the old man who perished "*in front of the main entrance of the Cathedral.*" There it was. I was right there, but once again, nothing. There was a monument for war heroes, but nothing on this poor Walter Myln. These two guys weren't as "lucky" as their two other fellows, Hamilton and Wishart, who had their names in fame.

William had only heard of these four. But there were other names in the book. I remembered well that martyrdom had happened in Market Street, because that was where I did my shopping.

So I went down Market Street, right next to the cathedral, looking down at the cobblestones until I reached the fountain. They must have been really old, as most of them were polished by use. It was hard to picture horses and carriages here, even less so a funeral pyre. This road was smack in the city center, the busiest one in town: cars going past, pedestrians walking around with their bags of purchases, mixed fragrances of perfume and fast food floating through the air. I saw no traces of a funeral pyre. What was really strange was that none of these martyrs died at the same place. I wondered why. I wanted to find out more about these men who'd perished. Why wasn't one of them mentioned on Martyr's Monument? Who was he again? How did all of this happen?

Lost in thought, I was ready to head home when I noticed a large cross on the ground. That was it. Up close, you couldn't see anything because it was big, but from afar... There was a huge Saint Andrew's cross made from red cobblestones on the gray road, much before you reached the fountain. I'd found it! Was this really for a martyr? It must have been, it was in the right place. I was happy I'd discovered it. I admired this cross for a while. People walked over it without hesitating, and most of them probably didn't even know why it was there. I'd have to dig deeper for the other martyrs.

I went to the library to see what I could find on this subject as they had some ancient books, and I was sure I'd get more accurate information than just googling. To begin with I had to discover what the cathedral looked like before falling into ruins so I could learn where the former doors were, especially the northern one.

I headed to the "local and regional history" section and stumbled on books with old photos of St Andrews, about the role of the Church or the Reform. Actually, there were quite a few books on this subject. Which one should I check out? I would never be able to read all of them! Leafing through a few volumes, I saw a picture of a reconstitution of the cathedral before it was destroyed and photocopied it.

I also took some notes on its history: starting with Saint Rule Church in 1120, where relics of Saint Andrew were once displayed. One tower was all that was now left of this 800-year-old church. Then, the construction of the cathedral and priory in 1160. In 1272 the nave had been destroyed by a storm and then the lead from the cathedral's roof had been dismantled to be melted into weapons for King Edward I of England. Robert the Bruce had consecrated it in 1318. At that time, the entire town benefitted from economic spinoffs with pilgrims from the whole country. But in 1378 the building had been damaged by a fire. A few years later part of the southern transept had fallen in yet another storm, and this had announced the beginning of the end for it. The cathedral had been abandoned with the Reform, and its furniture, statues and wealth had been all destroyed by Protestants. The roof had also been dismantled, then the central bell tower had toppled. Later the cathedral had been used as a cemetery before being renewed by the Marquis de Bute in 1893 and placed under state protection in 1946.

I looked through another book to find a better picture of the former cathedral. At that time, the main entrance, on the west, was monumental. There were two high turrets on that door. The stained-glass windows above them were also magnificent. It was the VIP entrance during ceremonies. Ordinary people used a smaller door, on the side. So that meant on the south or north! I was finally going to find my northern door! They said that you could still see traces of this entrance on the ground.

I noted all this information. I would go back to check if I could find it. Then I saw an etching of the cathedral before it was destroyed, on which paths were leading to secondary entrances. There wasn't just one door, but several. So that meant that the northern door must have been to the left, facing the sea.

I continued my research for slabs where the martyrs had perished, but found nothing. I yawned. It was time to go home, I was exhausted. My sleepless nights were negatively impacting my days.

I checked out a book on the cathedral and a few others on religious martyrs and left. It was already dark outside. How long had I been there? I absolutely had to gather up all the documents I'd recovered so I wouldn't lose any. Everything was finally starting to make sense. I felt like I had been given a mission: understanding what had happened in St Andrews. It would be tough, though, nearly impossible, but my curiosity had been aroused and now I was avid for details, I wanted to find out everything. My intellect had come across nourishment, as Mathieu wanted, and it was doing me good.

I slowly walked back to 7 Lochan Wynd, my mind still on my inquiries. I went inside the house and just one look at the guy's faces brought me back to reality immediately. William must have told Alex he'd found me with a knife. I put my stuff down and sat in an armchair across from them, ready to hear what they had to say.

Alex started.

"Anne, your attitude has been pretty strange lately, and I think you're too fragile to live in an environment like ours. Your insomnia, the accident in the bathroom, then last night when you disobeyed our house rules. And the knife! It's too dangerous for you, for us too. Everyone is worried."

He paused. I kept my eyes down, too uncomfortable to look them in the face.

"You've had some time to think about this. I turned things over in my head too. I am convinced that it would be a good idea, for all of us, if you left. We'll find you some other place to stay."

I raised my head and looked at William, who tried to justify this situation.

"It's for your own good. You'd be better off somewhere else. We could still see each other in town."

I couldn't believe that my friends had actually said that. Alex was right on some points, I had problems and I still hadn't overcome them. But was I the only person who had seen things in this house and in town? Why hadn't they told me about the house, the noise, and all that right from the start? Things did happen here; it wasn't just in my own head.

"I don't agree with your decision. I can explain it all... The reason why I was carrying a knife is that I found it under my pillow in Mathieu's room and I wanted him to tell me what it was doing there. He's the one you should talk about this. And as for locking the door, I'm frankly sorry. But how could I have known what would happen? Alex, you haven't been honest with me, you always let me believe that people told stories about the house and that they weren't true. But I know that things happen here. I'd like you to explain this once and for all."

They exchanged looks. A tense silence surrounded us. Had one of them put the knife under my pillow to scare me? Were they trying to make me go crazy? If so, why? I had the impression that they weren't the guys I'd met, the ones whom I drank beers with in the pub the night before—was it really the night before? I was losing track of time. They had changed and were now looking at me as if I were some sort of weird animal.

"Is the house accursed, Alex?"

I looked him in the eye, but he didn't answer. Suddenly Mathieu came in, slamming the door. I'd lost the opportunity to find out what was really happening.

"What the heck? You guys all look like death warmed over."

As no one replied anything, he pulled up a chair and sat down with us. I decided to start talking before Alex, to explain my version of the events that had taken place. When you admit things, the jury is usually more lenient...

"Mathieu, last night I found a knife under your pillow. That scared me and I went out looking for you, but you weren't there. William surprised me with the knife in my hand and he must have thought that I was trying to hurt you, or hurt myself, I don't know, but that scared him too. And when I went back to the room, I locked the door to feel safe."

I paused for a moment, and then I went on explaining the situation.

"The whole house responded to this affront, making the doors and windows slam. I 'disobeyed' the house rules and Alex is furious. He wants me to leave. Did you put that knife under my pillow?"

"No, it's not me, it's Rebecca."

"Rebecca?"

I was surprised. I'd thought about Mathieu, William and Alex, but not Rebecca. At the same time, that was logical: she was the one who encouraged me to go to the lake, she wanted to hurt me. Mathieu smiled. I kept on.

"Why would she do something like that?"

"It wasn't for you; it was for me. I didn't tell her we switched rooms. She says that it keeps evil spirits away and helps you sleep. She tried to take care of me in her own way."

Now I remembered—she had given me a carved pumpkin to "keep the evil spirits away." What kind of person was Rebecca? All of this was so strange. So the knife wasn't dangerous then. That also explained the way she looked at me the night before when I was in Mathieu's room. She was expecting to see him, not me. Alex spoke up.

"Okay, I think things are clear now. Anne, you can stay here if you want. But make sure you don't make any more mistakes that disturb the calm of this house. Never lock your door."

I was surprised at how quickly he'd changed his mind, as soon as Mathieu had arrived. Perhaps he was astonished that I'd stuck up for myself. I hadn't dared ask the question running through my head as I was afraid that he'd go back on his decision, but I swore that I'd ask Mathieu later to explain everything he knew about this house.

I picked up my stuff and went to my room, or Mathieu's room, should I have said. There was a red ribbon on the doorknob, I hadn't seen it the night before, and it looked like the one that had been hanging on the front door a while ago. Someone had been there. My shoes were no longer in the same place: now the heels were facing my bed. There was also a pair of my socks under the bed. Maybe Mathieu had been in to pick up some stuff. I had no idea when I'd be able to go back to my *real* room, the one overlooking the lake.

I picked up my documents. I was glad I'd found something to occupy my thoughts. I took out the map of St Andrews that I'd had since I arrived and decided to note what I'd discovered on it. The northern door of the cathedral must have been here, so I drew an N and I highlighted the outline of the cathedral before it fell into ruins. Then I tried to focus on the martyrs. I used the old book, *The City of St Andrews* for that.

I quickly located the part telling about the Protestant martyrs and looked for the name of the man who had perished in Market Street, the one whose cross I'd found earlier on the day. It was Pavel Kravar. Pavel Kravar? Never heard of him. I googled the name. I immediately found lots of information. Pavel Kravar was a Bohemian Czech. He'd studied medicine in Montpellier, then art in Paris and Prague, he became a physicist in Poland, then he went to Scotland to spread the Hussite movement, inspired by the doctrines of Jan Hus. Here he was known as Paul Craw. So Paul Craw was Pavel Kravar and had been burned to death in Market Street.

The other martyr, John Resby, perished in Perth, not in St Andrews. But Paul Craw's name wasn't on the city's monument. How come? Maybe because he'd died nearly a century before Hamilton? Or because he was a foreigner?

I took out a sheet of paper.

1433 – Paul Craw—Market Street

1528 – Patrick Hamilton—St Salvator Church

1533 – Henry Forrest—northern door of the cathedral

1546 – George Wishart—St Andrews Castle

1558 – Walter Myln—main entrance to the cathedral

On the map of St Andrews, I marked with an X each place where a martyr had died. It was easier now that I knew the town well. Then I looked at the result. The five marks were all on the tip of St Andrews, in the old town on the bay. Two crosses were pretty close to each other—Paul Craw's and Patrick Hamilton's. They were on the west. The others were all in very specific places, as if they were points on a compass. Forrest in the east, Wishart in the north, and Myln in the south. If you linked them all together, you'd have a diamond. Wonder if that meant something? I suddenly had an idea—drawing lines between the opposite points. That way I drew a cross, in the alignment of the cathedral.

I was proud of what I'd discovered. A cross! This must have been intentional. I had no idea why, but everything matched. If only I could talk about this to William, the history buff, see what was his opinion. But now he was so distant. What had I done to him? Why didn't he trust me anymore? I was disappointed that he'd betrayed me with Alex and that both of them had decided I had to leave. Luckily for me Mathieu came! That saved me. I had to talk to him, I had so many questions. Where had he been last night? What did he know about the house? Where had he found that old book that was in the library? I had confided in him, telling him about my solitude and despair, he was the only one who understood me. I realized I needed to share my discoveries with him, be near him to justify my acts and validate, if I could use that word, my presence here.

I looked out the window. There was a light on in Rebecca's room. I thought of the knife again. So she was the one who had put it under Mathieu's pillow! How strange. Mathieu was convinced she wanted to protect him ... but from what? What was dangerous here? I didn't really trust her. She'd said she wanted to distance the evil spirits from me with that pumpkin, but I almost drowned. What was she trying to do? Maybe she knew stuff about the house too? Why didn't anyone say anything to me? I'd have to find answers to my questions by myself.

Suddenly the light went off in the room across the street. A few seconds later, Rebecca walked out and closed the door behind her. She was wearing a long dark dress. I immediately ran down the stairs and followed her discreetly. She was taking the path leading to the woods and lakes. At this time of night? Weird. I waited a bit so she wouldn't see me and then hurried so I wouldn't lose sight of her. We had already left the road and arrived at the path. Light from the street lights was now far away and it was pitch-black without it. I was afraid that she'd hear me, so I was careful with each and every step.

Rebecca turned on a flashlight. Was I ever stupid! I'd left in such a hurry that I didn't even think of taking one! Little by little my eyes would get used to the darkness, but for now, I couldn't see much of anything. I followed her to the best of my ability, but she was walking faster than I was. I had to catch up with her so I accelerated. The path turned into a narrow trail. I could picture the dark mass of the trees in the background, as well as the lake. What could she be doing here in the middle of the night? I shivered. I could see her nearing the lake, though I'd hoped she wouldn't go that far.

My heart started to pound and my stomach knotted up. I was afraid. Afraid of this place, afraid of what it had done to me. Huffing and puffing, I continued to follow her. I could see a beam of light slowly swaying about fifty feet in front of me, creating a halo on the ground, but I couldn't actually distinguish anything. But I knew where we were and didn't need to actually see. A huge mass of unmoving and cold water was lying beyond. I slowed down. Did I really want to follow her there? I remembered what Mathieu had said.

"Rebecca never goes near water, she's afraid of it."

If this was really true, she wouldn't be walking here in the middle of the night. What was she hiding?

Suddenly the flashlight was turned off. Had she heard me? As I couldn't make out anything, I stopped. Now what? I couldn't believe that I was dumb enough to have followed her here. I presumed she'd stopped right before the woods, but how could I be sure? I couldn't let her catch me. I tried to imagine what she could be doing here in the woods at this time of night. Meeting someone maybe? Digging a hole to hide something? But in that case, she wouldn't have turned her lamp off. Unless she had seen me and was trying to ditch me. On one of those nights when I wasn't able to sleep, I did recognize a feminine silhouette leaving the woods early in the morning. I remembered seeing long black hair. Perhaps it was Rebecca.

My face and hands were freezing now. I decided to turn back, slowly, though I was disappointed. I wouldn't learn anymore tonight.

Everything was calm in the house. No one in the living room, nor in the bedrooms apparently. Maybe the guys had gone out for a drink. I sighed. I would have liked to join them, try to ignore what had happened between us. I felt further and further away from Alex and couldn't forget the way William had looked at me, with strange and nearly unforgiving eyes. How could things have changed so much in such a short time?

I kept asking myself questions, over and over again. I'd have to calm down if I wanted to get some sleep tonight. I went upstairs and lay down on my bed.

Looking up at the ceiling, I saw a strange drawing. I stood up on the bed so I could observe it better. It looked like a Celtic pattern. It was a circle drawn with a black marker, with three arcs, almost three petals you could say, that joined each other in the middle of the circle. Or three petals with a ring on top of them.

I remembered seeing this somewhere before, but I couldn't pinpoint.

Rebecca must have drawn this to protect Mathieu once again from the evil spirits. How many protections had she put in his room? What was so dangerous in this house? This was not very reassuring.

I lay back down on the bed and picked the old book up that

was on my table. Even if I'd often looked through it, I still hadn't read every page. What an interesting book. So much information in it! Once again, I wondered how Mathieu got it. The cover didn't have a title on it and many of the pages were dog-eared. Upon examining it closely, I could see that the binding was coming loose too. A book this old... I had to do something about that. In an angle, inside the book, I tugged gently on the cover to see how bad the damage was. Then I realized that there was a second binding beneath it. I took off the first thick layer of paper, inch by inch. Little by little I could see a beautiful leather-bound book. I didn't believe my eyes! I delicately took this layer of paper off, then cleaned it carefully to get the traces of glue off. Why would someone hide such a beautiful binding? I smiled, proud of myself, as if I had made a great discovery. Mathieu would be happy when I gave him this book back, now that it had its soul and authenticity once again.

I opened the book to read it when a sheet of mildewed paper slipped from its pages and fell at my feet. I picked it up: it was an old letter written in brown ink. I eagerly read the spidery handwriting.

"I'm dying because I bother
Those around me
Those people without parsimony
Do the same to me!
I hate the wind and the rain;
I hate the heat and the cold;
I therefore abandon my life
Without regrets and without fear. Please forgive me."

140

A name and a date on the bottom of the page: Margaret, 1914.

Margaret? Who was she? What a sad little text. I immediately thought about Baudelaire's poetry where he also expressed spleen and tedium. What could have happened for her to be so weary and disgusted with life?

Please forgive me... These last words were the worst of all, as if this Margaret was going to commit suicide.

Everything was mixed up in my head. All the mysterious stuff in this house, my work on the martyrs in St Andrews, the authentic cover of the book and this poignant testimonial from an unknown person. My head was about to explode.

It was too much for me. I stepped out to see if the guys were back, but no lights were on. I felt alone. I walked onto the landing, my pupils dilated in the dark. Without being able to explain why, I had to go into my room overlooking the lake. I opened the door and entered. Moonlight came in through the window, giving the objects chimeric outlines. I basked in the moment of enjoying being there, in this room that had seen so many things. I was strangely very calm. Little by little, I could make out minute movements, an indistinct effusion, uncertain vibrations. Sort of like when you see a shooting star, everything goes so fast that you wonder if you'd imagined it. Things were happening and I was surrounded, but they were so fast that I couldn't distinguish anything. Misty shadows and movements of immobile air. I knew that they were there and now I started to notice their presence. I tried to convey a feeling of peace to them, it seemed to work as they weren't aggressive. We accepted each other. There nonetheless was a difference between us: they knew me, whereas I didn't know them. I tried to ask them who they were. No one answered.

I lay down on the bed and little by little fell asleep. I could visualize the lake and woods. Someone was looking at me, someone I couldn't see.

The trees in the forest were full of shadows, shadows no one could see. They were there in sunlight, in moonlight. They were light and they moved. I could remain for hours or day on end, looking at them. They didn't speak, they never stopped moving, they never died. They remained behind the trees, behind these huge oaks with their leaves, steadfast against the wind, impervious to rain. Then they suddenly looked at me, all of these shadows behind the trees. They didn't like being looked at.

I was sitting on the PH cobblestones. I heard tired voices.

"Anne, help me."

I was tiny, as if an invisible weight was on my chest, and each of them was coming to me, Hamilton, Myln, Craw, Wishart. Each of them was asking me for help.

"Anne, help me. I'm begging you."

Their faces were horrible and bloody, their voices mere moans, their presence unbearable... But they kept coming up to me, one after another, looking at me, speaking louder and louder.

"Anne! Help us, Anne! We're dying."

Margaret was with them. Now their rhythm was picking up speed, I barely had time to see them and hear them crying out and the next one was already there.

"Anne!"

"Anne!"

Hearing my name like that became painful. One of them grabbed me, another one squeezed my arm, then another one touched my face with his scorched hand, before going down my neck. I was suffocating. I wanted to get this hand off my throat, the hand that was squeezing me, asphyxiating me.

I opened my eyes suddenly. Faces were looking at me. What were these people doing in my room? I found it hard to breathe. One of them came closer, and I immediately recognized him, I couldn't forget his swollen eyes. Patrick Hamilton. I woke up with a jolt, out of breath.

— CHAPTER NINE —

"One large salt-and-vinegar chips. Coming up."

I went to the kitchen to give the cook the order. I had already done the cleaning upon arriving this morning. In the restroom, the "Now Wash Your Hands" sign made me smile. Washing your hands, that should come naturally, you didn't need a sign for that... A bit before noon, customers began walking in. I was a little nervous as most people didn't speak French and I was afraid I wouldn't understand everyone. I hadn't actually met too many Scottish people since I'd been there, and they did have a heavy accent. Besides, I'd never worked as a waitress.

Adam served the beverages and I served the meals. It wasn't packed and most customers had a quick bite, or just ordered sandwiches to go. In spite of that, I was really busy. Taking orders, going to the kitchen, the heat, waiting on tables. It was a lot for a beginner. I was exhausted. I almost spilled a boiling plate but managed not to at the very last second. I hadn't slept well again last night without remembering what I had dreamed of.

After the lunch hour rush, I sorted the dishes and waste. All these plates, all this food, a vicious consumption circle! I did the dishes, dried them so they'd be really clean, put the plates and glasses away and cleaned the tables with a sanitizer. I had been far from imagining such hard work. I nonetheless was satisfied: I hadn't had a minute to think about what was happening at home. All this activity emptied my brain. And with a little luck, I'd be able to sleep better at night, seeing how much I ran around during the day!

I had a couple of hours to kill before going back to work, but preferred not to return to Lochan Wynd for now, as I didn't want to run across Alex.

I ordered a pizza to go and went to the beach, admiring the waves, seagulls and the town on the cliff. It was strange to be there, while knowing that this "there" wouldn't last. Each day I would get up, conscious that my stay would come to an end, as I was the one who had chosen the date. I'd be leaving and never seeing them again.

I'd be returning home. But where was my real home? Lochan Wynd had become my home now and I wasn't sure I wanted to leave it. A home is a place where you *live*, and I didn't feel alive anymore when I was in Pélissanne, in France. It was becoming harder and harder to know why I had to fly back in just a few weeks. This wasn't really an exile for me, I liked being there. I forgot the past, I began to lose touch with reality, lose my marks, my identity…

In fact, for that very reason, I had to go back, so I wouldn't lose myself completely. This exile was like opium, it had cured me at first before making me addicted to it and becoming someone else. I had to be careful. France was the trunk with my roots in it, and if I wanted to find myself, I would have to return to my country and my former life, see my friends and family, do what I used to do. Got it. That was why I had to leave Scotland.

But I couldn't leave things unfinished, my questions had to be answered before. What was taking place at the lakefront? What was in the house? Why was I so obsessed with these Protestant martyrs?

I was exhausted. I closed my eyes for an instant that lasted nearly an hour.

I had the map where I'd put an X where each martyr had perished, then drawn in a cross, linking them all together that faced the east, aligned with St Andrews Cathedral. I still wasn't sure that my research would actually lead to anything, but I wanted to keep on trying up to the very end, as if all of these elements had personally affected me. It had become an obsession. I still had some time left before my evening shift at The Drinking Bastards. I wanted to check where the northern door in the cathedral was located. If it was where I believed it would be, I'd find traces of Henry Forrest's funeral pyre there.

I pulled my hat down to cover my frozen ears and, hands in my pockets, walked towards East Sands. Winter was on its way, in the morning you could already see heavy white frost on the grass along the road. The breeze was colder and colder. Night was also falling earlier now and I knew that it would be dark in an hour. I could make out the two layered towers of the cathedral, and soon was at the foot of the monument. I was hunting for traces on the ground that would show me where the former northern door was.

I took the photocopy of the etching of the renovated cathedral in 1828 out of my pocket: this drawing was done well after the Protestant martyrdom, yet gave me a good idea of what the cathedral had looked like when it was still standing proudly. I could imagine the inhabitants coming to mass, with their Sunday best, the ladies wearing long dresses and intricate hats. The main door, facing west, was still impressive, with a high tower on the right side, the only one still standing. I could picture the copper-colored roof shining in the sun, illuminating the inhabitants of St Andrews, making the cathedral visible even from Scores Road, like a light at the end of a tunnel.

I humbly went into what was the cathedral's former nave: on the ground I could make out the places where the stone columns had been and was impressed by their size. There must have been twenty of them, standing in a row from front to back. The entire right side of the cathedral was still standing, touching what used to be the priory, and I could see where the stained-glass windows must have been, whereas the left wall had crumbled down completely.

A bit farther on there was a former well, that had now been filled in. A well? Maybe to have an unlimited supply of holy water. Or maybe back then the whole town got their water inside the cathedral. I turned around and walked next to the northern wall, and in just a few steps I was able to see traces of a passage, with some ancient foundations. I was pretty sure of myself here, this was what I had been looking for! I examined my drawing: I was sure now: this was where the northern door of the cathedral had been located.

Now there were gravestones right when you went outside, but there must have been a church square there before, where that poor Forrest had been burned alive. I unfortunately didn't see any initials like for Hamilton or Wishart that marked the exact spot that would have proved this.

I felt a breath of cold air on my neck and quickly turned around. I caught sight of a shadow, or should I say a vague light sliding along the wall before it disappeared. I thought of the White Lady, the one who Ben and Donald told me haunted this cathedral. Should I be afraid? These stories couldn't be true.

I focused back to my drawing; it was right then. If Forrest died here and you linked the other places of the funeral pyres together, you had a Latin cross. What was really strange was that none of these martyrs perished at the same place. I wondered why. And did that cross mean anything? Hard to say. I didn't have an overview, because I could only see one thing at a time from where I was. I was being too down to earth here, too focused on traces on the ground. I had to step back some, maybe take a look from the top to understand all of this.

I looked up from my drawing. There were some tourists there, taking pictures. They were ridiculous, hiding their heads beneath their hoods, trying to resist Scottish elements with their waterproof jackets, completely frozen. When you go on vacation someplace, you think you'll be alone, but you're always wrong. One of them walked up to me. I pretended not to see him and turned around, but I had been too slow and the foreigner, who was already next to me now, asked me a question in his pitiful English that he'd learned in France.

"Excuz-me."

I looked at him so he would finish.

"Canne you take ... photography of us?"

I nodded and smiled, grabbing his camera. He was delighted I'd understood him and quickly joined his friends who all congratulated him on his verbal excellence. They took their hoods off for the photo and all smiled, then just after the flash quickly put them right back on while complaining about the lousy weather that was spoiling their vacations and above all, would make all their souvenir photos look sad.

"Sank you very meuch. Euh... We from France. Euh... Ze weazer is bad..."

The tourist pointed at the sky where a heavenly combat was taking place between several shades of gray. I knew what he tried to say: it was raining, windy and cold. There was mud all over and no one was in the streets. I could tell he was struggling to express himself in English, but I didn't help him. Firstly, I didn't want him to know that I was also French, and secondly, I didn't want to spoil his sterling reputation in front of his friends.

"Euh... Zut, comment on dit déjà... Euh... We want to euh ... go tower, possibeul?"

I didn't know that you could visit St Rule Tower. I took them to the fence at the bottom of the tower, where there was an urn with a sign on it. "Thank you for your participation in the maintenance expenses for our Tower."

With my nearly perfect English, I explained to them that while you could visit the tower, you were expected to contribute to its upkeep and leave some spare change. Not only did they not notice I also had a French accent (and believe me, everyone else did!), but they didn't understand one word of what I was telling them, and I had to reformulate my sentence with simpler words. The proverbial light finally came on in their brains and they climbed the century-old stairs.

After a few minutes, I could no longer hear them. The iron gate was creaking in the wind. Night had just fallen, the sun had set even earlier than the day before, about 4 p.m. I wanted to see the view from the top of the tower. A person wearing a city uniform walked up to me: she was a tour guide. I nodded when she asked me if I wanted more information about this monument. That day was November 30th, the Saint Andrew patron saint day, and the city sponsored free tours of the castle and cathedral.

"Many years ago the tower was attached to a chapel, St Regulus Chapel. We don't know who really built it nor when, but legends say that a Pict called Hergust built this chapel to bear witness to his devotion to God around the fourth century, making it the oldest building in St Andrews. This chapel housed the relics of Saint Andrew and was the last resting place of the many clerics who were buried here. Other historical events impacting St Andrews also took place in Saint Rule. For example, in 1547 cannons were placed on top of the tower, aiming at the castle in order to oust Norman Leslie, who, with the help of Henry VIII, had taken possession of it. Another interesting anecdote, St Rule Tower is also famous for its ghost that can be seen on the top of the tower. It's the ghost of Prior Robert de Montrose, who liked to go up to the top of the tower to admire the view. Everyone appreciated him, except one monk whom he had scolded and thrown into the priory's dungeon for having flirted with a woman. One night, the monk snuck up behind Robert de Montrose when he was on top of the tower, stabbed him in revenge and threw him off. Ever since then, the Prior's ghost can often be observed around the tower, wearing his Augustinian habit and hood, overlooking the town."

"Thank you for all your explanations. Do you know if this ghost is related to the White Lady?"

"No, not at all, except that they both 'haunt' the cathedral. Sometimes the White Lady can be seen around the Abbey Wall Tower. She was one of the 'Marys', one of Mary Stuart's servants and was in love with Pierre de Châtelard, a French poet, who loved the beautiful Mary Stuart. It was considered an affront when he confessed his passion to the queen. He was thrown into one of the dungeons and sentenced to die the next morning. Mary, the servant, tried to convince him to leave the country and helped him escape, but he refused. She spent the whole night roaming between the cathedral and castle, hoping he'd change his mind. But when daylight broke, it was too late and Pierre de Châtelard was taken to Market Cross in Market Street and beheaded in 1562. Young Mary entered into the orders and finally died of a broken heart. Ever since that time she can still be seen, roaming between the castle and cathedral, dressed in white."

So the White Lady story was true then, Ben and Donald hadn't lied to me, except when they added the detail of the terrifying face the nun had. Market Cross... That's where Paul Craw had been burned at the stake.

"What exactly is Market Cross?"

"It was like a little covered marketplace right in the center of town and that was where everything that was important took place. That's where Craw preached in 1433; Châtelard was beheaded there, like I said; Robert Blair gave a speech supporting the inhabitants of St Andrews during the plague. Then Market Cross fell into ruins and was destroyed in 1768. All that's left today is a cross on the cobblestones."

"Can I go up on top of the Tower?"

"Sure, but don't stay too long, I'm going to close soon and it's dangerous when it's dark."

"Thank you!"

I put a coin in the urn and started walking up the narrow stairs. I came across the French guys who were coming down. After roughly a hundred steps, I arrived on top, out of breath, both because of the number of stairs as well as the view.

I could see the town of St Andrews on the west with its gray stone houses, even the shadows of people walking in the street and the headlights of the cars. On the east, you saw the dark blue water in the bay, with boats bobbing up and down in the waves and the white foam of the saltwater. Farther away, on the horizon, there was a lighthouse sweeping the sky with its light. And below me, the dark ruins of the cathedral, mixing their dust with that of the bodies buried there. I dominated the entire city from here. I took my drawing out, the wind wrinkled it. I wanted to see where the central point was in the lines of the cross I'd drawn. One finger on my map, looking down at the town, I finally found where they met: it was on one side of North Street, more exactly at the first house with a red roof after the two gray ones coming from the cathedral, next to a garden overlooking the Scores and the castle.

"Miss? I have to close now."

"Coming!"

One last look at the view that Robert de Montrose loved so much and I went down the stairs, making sure I didn't slip on the moist and smooth steps.

I thanked the guide who closed the metallic gate behind me. I glanced at my watch; it was nearly five. Shoot! I was going to be late for work!

I ran off, waving at the municipal employee. Behind me a pale and sad moon was coming up.

Adam told me I was a bit late tonight and immediately gave me some orders of fries he'd taken and that were ready. These Scots sure ate early! As it already was dark out, you thought it was night, whereas in France at five p.m. you'd feel like you were in the middle of the afternoon...

I rushed into the kitchen where it smelled of hot oil and came out all shiny as if I'd taken a Turkish bath, two plates of fries in my hands.

"There you go!"

"*Merci beau cul²!*"

I stopped in my tracks.

"Excuse me?"

"*Merci beau cul.* Isn't that how you say it in French?"

"Oh yeah. Almost, but with an 'ou' at the end: *merci beaucoup.*"

Two chicken burgers, nuggets, one vegetarian cheeseburger, three cheddar paninis, nachos, a baked potato with tuna. Orders were pouring in. A lot of people ate alone, drinking a pint. It was a whirlwind, I flew from table to table, from the kitchen to the bar, until 8 p.m. where I began my evening duties at the bar serving our many customers.

"Adam, can you make me a 'holy cow' please? Thanks!"

He prepared the cocktails I didn't know how to and I served beer, whisky, and soft drinks. Both of us were busy behind the

---

² Thank you, nice ass.

bar. The background noise was deafening, people were crowded in front of us and had to yell out their orders so we could hear them. We couldn't even hear the music anymore, just conversations and laughter.

"Hello. You recognize us? We at ze cathedral this afternoon!"

I raised my head and saw that the French tourists had unfortunately found me again. I just smiled. They ordered glasses of Guinness, which I served, of course, in accordance with the instructions though I knew they wouldn't comply with the six points on the poster. When they left, I noticed none of them had finished their drinks, they probably didn't like how this unique beer tasted.

I served glasses of Gordon, Guinness, Boddingtons, Deuchars, an Australian chardonnay, and later that night vodka, rum, and lots of whisky. Glasses emptied themselves nearly as fast as we served them. Money passed from hand to hand, then into the cash register, as if the customers were trying to purchase our silence on their alcoholic habits. And all this lasted until late in the night.

— CHAPTER TEN —

Days were flying by. This new job at the pub filled up my days and during my free time, I continued my research. I wasn't always at home and spent lots of time wandering up and down the roads in St Andrews, looking at the passersby and peering at the walls and cobblestones in the town still searching for clues. I felt as if I'd found something that was key in this affair, but without really knowing what.

Despite the distance I felt between us, I shared my work with William. He was interested in the history of the city, and he was the one who told me about the slabs and their meaning. I showed him my drawing, with the cross that linked the four places where those martyrs had perished, right in line with the cathedral. The Hamilton—Forrest line superimposed itself on the nave and the Wishart—Myln line on the transepts.

I was satisfied with myself, because I'd progressed so much in English and could now speak nearly fluently. The explanations of my inquiries seemed to be coherent. Now I answered easily in English without even thinking about it and sometimes dreamed in English too.

William unfortunately didn't have the reaction I had been hoping for. He was much less enthusiastic than I was about what I'd found out for the martyrs, even saying that this was all pure nonsense. Besides, he was quite patronizing about all my work that was keeping me up night and day. I now felt a bit of suspicion, a coldness that distanced him from me. I no longer recognized the William I'd known and that made me sad.

Alex avoided me and when we came across each other, he was indifferent. I was conscious he had wanted me to leave and that he wasn't happy that I was still here. We lived together without passion, but in peace.

The only real friend I had left was Mathieu. I had sincerely thanked him for having allowed me to remain at Lochan Wynd. But I saw him less and less often: either he wasn't at home, or he was busy, or he was with Rebecca.

Despite the lack of support from William, I continued my investigations, but alone. That was all I could think of now, and I wanted to solve this puzzle before leaving. William wasn't open-minded enough to realize how important this work was. I was about to uncover one of the mysteries of the cornerstones of St Andrews, one that would make everything else clear. This revelation would be indispensable to each inhabitant of the city, allowing them to understand the historical wealth of the streets they walked on every day. Nothing was random, some sort of superior being had necessarily planned everything and I was going to find the key that opened that door. And by solving this riddle, I hoped to rid myself of the shadows I saw at night, while I was at it.

My troubled spirit was always in motion so I couldn't rest. With the fatigue I'd accumulated for months now, I was constantly in a trance. All that kept me going was coffee, cigarettes and my nerves. I couldn't stand my reflection in the mirror, these dark rings under my hollow eyes. I only slept for three to four hours a night, and had nightmares and visions of martyrs. At work, I dozed off if I was inactive for too long forcing Adam to nudge me with his elbow to wake me up. I quickly became impatient with my clients who'd had too much to drink, I found it hard to remember their orders and sometimes made mistakes giving them change. Besides, I was tormented by horrible migraines. At night I was afraid I'd never fall asleep, and that made me toss and turn in bed—or should I say Mathieu's—as I still was in his room. And when I couldn't close my eyes, I either read or logged onto my laptop. One night I even started counting the words in Mathieu's English-French dictionary. On the first page, they said there were 56,000 words. How could they prove it? I decided to check. But after 2,458 words on the 41st page, my eyes were tingling and I began to make mistakes. Half asleep, I started to see strange things: this sign on the ceiling—the circle with the three overlapping ovals—obsessed me and I could feel as if it was observing me with its three eyes. I often smelled an odor of something burning, I heard frightening whispers, the first names of the martyrs: Paul, Patrick, George, Walter and Henry...

So I pulled Lara's photo out from under my pillow, then photos of Guillaume and my parents to calm down. I had to fight for them.

All of this had to end. Once I solved this mystery, I'd find peace. I thought back on the house with the red roof tiles on North Street, the culmination of all my research. I'd gone by it many times: a stone facade and white windows with small windowpanes, and a blue door with Number 17 marked on it. On the right, there was an iron gate with a sign "15 North Street & Marine Place" on it that seemed to lead to the gardens behind the house. I knew an elderly man lived here.

One afternoon, I decided to ring the bell on the blue door. I had to talk to this man, he perhaps had the key that could solve this riddle.

"Come in! It's open!"

I turned the doorknob, and it wasn't locked. I remained outside, not seeing anyone.

"Ye're early Lorna. I wasnae expectin' ye until teatime," continued a weak voice.

"Um, hello. I'm not Lorna, Sir."

"Who are ye then? What's yer name?"

"You don't know me, my name is Anne."

"One moment please. I'll be down in a wee while."

I waited forever. My eyes had the time to examine the interior decoration, my nose to breathe in the scent of mothballs, my back to rest against the blue door.

I finally saw an old man emerge, carefully coming down the stairs. He was wheezing and out of breath. However, he was freshly shaved, his hair had gel to hold it in place, and in spite of his age, his silhouette led me to believe he took good care of himself.

"Hello Lass. What can I do fur ye?"

"Sir, I was wondering if I could ask you a few questions. It might seem strange. Questions about the cathedral. You live right next to it and ... well, maybe I'm wrong here, but I thought you could tell me lots of things ... things that would be useful in my research."

"Are ye preparin' a thesis fur the university?"

"Um, yes, you could put it like that."

"Did Professor Barlett send ye?"

"No, I came to you alone."

He took out his pocket watch—that must have been a hundred years old! Things like that still existed?

"We dinnae have a lot o' time; it'll be teatime in less than two hours."

"I don't want to disturb you."

"At my age, visits are always welcome ye know. Come in Lass, this way."

We sat down in his living room. There were loaded

bookshelves behind the sofa, and a diploma in Local History issued by the University of St Andrews in 1950 to a certain John Forrest. He settled into an armchair and slowly exhaled several times to get his breath back. That made a very unpleasant sound, as if water were boiling inside his lungs.

"Mr. Forrest, thank you so much for seeing me. I'm very grateful to you. Are you related to that unfortunate Henry Forrest?"

"Nae at all Lass, though I spent years o' my life studyin' him."

"Actually I'm working on the martyrs in St Andrews. I'm sure I can learn a lot from you: I found a slab that marked the place where Hamilton perished, the PH cobblestone, the GW cobblestone and Paul Craw's paved cross on Market Street too. But I didn't find anything that showed where Myln or Forrest died."

"Ye're right, neither o' them has a slab, but sometimes there's a cairn there."

"A cairn?"

"Aye, a heap o' stones. A few days after the execution, some people built a cairn where the martyr perished, to honor his memory. These cairns were replaced by slabs fur famous martyrs, like Patrick Hamilton or George Wishart. Fur Myln and Forrest, the cairn was often destroyed, then rebuilt, but never transformed into an eternal slab. Still today, unknown people come an' add a stone to their cairns. They are centuries old, an' the memory o' the martyrs is still there."

A pile of stones! That was why I never noticed anything! This old professor knew what he was talking about! But that didn't tell me why the epicenter of my diagram was his house. After a few painful inspiration and expiration, John continued.

"Ye're nae takin' any notes? The cathedral is an important place. The three main roads in St Andrews lead to it. It represents the Church, beliefs, a supreme power. The Church tormented many people in St Andrews, nae just the martyrs. Have ye been to the mound where the Martyr's Monument is located, near the sea, at the bottom o' North Street?"

"Yes, I went there for my research."

"Before, this mound used to be called 'The Witches' Mountain.' There werenae just Protestants who were accused o' heresy. Once the Reform was in place an' Protestantism was established, they found other people to persecute: witches. There were witch hunts throughout the seventeenth century. Thousands o' people were accused o' bein' witches in Scotland an' about thirty o' them were burned at the stake here in St Andrews, most o' them women; the last one to die was Young, in 1667. She stayed right here in North Street. A couple o' hundred years before, we would have been neighbors."

He paused and took a drink of water. Neither of us spoke. His breathing was like a grandfather's clock swinging. It was a bit after three.

"Everything you're telling me is really interesting, Mr.

163

Forrest. Can you tell me a bit more about North Street?"

"At the end o' the nineteenth century, a lot o' fishermen lived here in North Street, a tightly-knit an' independent community. They were hard workers an' life wasnae easy fur them. Often the sea was rough, an' many o' them perished. Their wives could often be seen sittin' at their front doors, repairin' their nets. Boats came into the port with their loads o' potatoes, salt, or coal. The lighthouse at the end o' the wharf didnae prevent all the shipwrecks, though. People went to the wharf to watch the rescuers, such as John Honey, a student, who in 1800 took all the crew from the *Janet Macduff* back to shore, one by one. An act o' bravery remembered fur generations on."

The elderly man continued to talk, with his pained breathing as a background. He loved telling me all this, but still hadn't answered my question. I preferred not to unveil my discoveries directly, although I really wanted to know why his house was at the center of my diagram. I tried to put him back on track.

"Mr. Forrest, at the time when all of these poor martyrs died, North Street was an important road, wasn't it?"

"Aye, it was, North Street an' South Street were like boulevards bringin' the pilgrims to the cathedral: ye can tell by the width o' the street how important it was in the Middle Ages. At this time, North Street was called 'NorthGait' an' it had loads o' little chapels on it."

"Your house looks really old. And it's right next to the cathedral. Do you know if it has anything to do with the martyrs? Perhaps one of them lived here?"

"What a strange question. I have no idea. I've stayed here since 1945. I moved here after the war, before that I stayed in Lochan Wynd."

"Lochan Wynd?"

"Aye Lochan Wynd."

Unbelievable. He'd lived in Lochan Wynd! Everything was linked. Questions were popping up in my head, but I didn't want to rush the old man. I responded enthusiastically.

"I know that place well, and I'm living at number 7!"

I'd presumed he'd find that interesting too, but he looked away from me suddenly. I cleared my throat and continued the conversation.

"What a strange coincidence. What number was your house?"

He didn't answer, locked in his memories. The tick-tock of the clock filled the silence, covered by his throaty breathing.

"Mr. Forrest?"

"Um? Er, excuse me. Old memories... Um... Lochan Wynd, from the Scottish word 'Wynd', a narrow road an' 'Lochan,' a wee loch. Hmm."

His head was bobbing up and down slowly. His lips were pursed, his eyes squinted, as if he were thinking hard.

"Did you know the people who lived at Number 7?"

He had a faint smile, still nodding.

"O' course. But that doesnae have anythin' to do with yer research, Lassie."

"Oh please, tell me about them! Did you know Elizabeth?"

"Elizabeth? Aye, I did. That was a long time ago though. We lived next to one another, I was a young lad at the time."

Suddenly the door opened and our conversation was interrupted.

"John?"

Mr. Forrest glanced over at the clock and explained.

"That's Lorna, fur cuppa."

I knew I wouldn't get anything else from him at the moment. I was invited to stay for tea, but politely refused.

"Come back an' see me next week, Lassie, we'll continue our little talk."

"Thank you!"

And I left the two of them for their traditional teatime. It was already dark outside. The sun had set; the overcast sky made for a grim atmosphere.

The Drinking Bastards Pub was packed because of a soccer match: everyone who was anyone must have been there to watch it. Adam shouted at me, while preparing drinks.

"Anne, do you mind doing extra hours? I think you'll have

to stay until closing time tonight."

"Sure, no problem."

I was a partner-in-crime to what had gone on in the past few days: money for alcoholic pleasures. After chugging down a few pints, men began to change. They spoke loudly, laughed at nothing at all, told the same jokes over and over and sputtered when they asked for refills. Then they took one another by the shoulders and began singing. After one too many glasses, some of them ended up sleeping, their heads on the tables. In the worst case, a fight would break out and Adam would take out his foghorn to make those involved go outside.

As for the girls, things were not much better. Classy when they came in, they ended up with red eyes and drizzly mascara. Their cleavage increased as time went by. The most talented ones ended up on the knees of their prey, strutting their stuff under their noses. Others broke down sobbing or ran to the toilets to vomit.

I noticed a Mohawk hairdo in the crowd. It was Pete, our neighbor, Rebecca's brother. He leaned on the counter, already drunk, and ordered a pint of Tennents®, our cheapest beer. I didn't even know if he'd recognized me. "I'm drinking to forget..."

I served him his pint, and as it had momentarily calmed down, I stood in front of him and listened.

"I got expelled because of my grades. If they don't improve, I'm going to lose my scholarship. And then I'll have to pay back all my tuition fees, shit! As I don't have a penny to my name, I'll barely be able to pay for my first semester and I'll have to leave this university and find a cheaper one. If I continue, that is."

He took a huge swallow of beer and without looking at me, carried on talking.

"I'm screwed! Rebecca had warned me... But it's too hard. I don't know how she does it. She's so strong! I don't want to do anything anymore. I hate my courses. I keep thinking of her. Of before. I remember how on Sunday mornings she'd make porridge and pancakes for us, just wearing her bathrobe, without even having combed her hair ...'

"Who was that?"

"My mom."

He didn't continue, nor did I, surprised by this declaration. I heard the last word resonate in my head, over and over. His mother? I'd thought he was talking about one of his girlfriends. Perhaps behind all his eccentricity—Mohawk hairdo, tattoos— he was hiding a deep wound and a damaged personality.

Two tittering blonds sashayed up to the counter.

"Hi. What can we drink with ... this?"

And hilarious, they emptied out their wallets on the bar. There was just petty change, and some of the coins even rolled to the floor. I counted them—less than £1.50.

"Not much, sorry. You don't have enough."

"Come on, please... You're young, you know what it's like

when you don't have much money, otherwise you wouldn't be working here. Can we have a Rum-Coke?"

"I can't. It's not my bar, I'm just the waitress."

"How about a small glass, and half filled with rum? Could you do that? Like the dose of rum for £1.50?"

"Okay girls."

"Thanks, you're too nice!"

And I poured them a glass, full sized, and gave them some change. Adam would never notice he was missing an inch of rum in the bottle and I'm sure my little arrangement wouldn't impact his bottom line.

Adam told me we were no longer serving drinks and it was time for people to head home so we could clean up and close. I nodded and started collecting the empty glasses on the tables.

Pete was still there, silent, staring into space. I was picking up the glasses in front of him, and he continued to speak.

"My mother died. Two years ago. That was in July, we were at West Sands Beach, it was hot. We even went swimming. My mom went to town, she had something to do and said she'd join us later. We waited, but she never came back. We finally got dressed and returned home. In front of the aquarium, we saw a group of people and a rescue squad. We stopped to see what was going on. They'd found a body on the beach. She'd fallen from the cliffs when she took a shortcut to go back to West Sands, almost forty feet. Fuck, this body under the white cloth was my mother..."

He paused.

"I still wonder why she went there. There was a sign and a fence so people wouldn't walk there, and you could see there wasn't even a path, just a steep slope towards nothing. Since then life has been tough. My father drinks like a fish and never leaves his couch. Rebecca releases her pain through her painting. She sometimes has crazy reactions, even scaring me. As for me, I've become a lazy bum—can't even keep up with classes at the university."

"I'm so sorry. I had no idea about your mom."

I'd always thought that Rebecca and her brother lived together, sharing a flat like most students here. I didn't realize their dad lived with them. I'd never seen him. Why didn't Mathieu tell me this? He was really close to Rebecca.

Adam rang the closing bell. Little by little people left.

"Pete, we're closing now. Are you going to be okay?"

He nodded, but I could see he wasn't doing well at all, especially emotionally. I didn't know what to do with him, but I couldn't leave him, not after what he'd just confided in me.

"We can go back home together, if you want. Give me fifteen? I just have to wash the tables and we can go."

"Okay, cool."

I wiped down half the tables to get the sticky alcohol traces off, while Adam did the same thing on the other side. Then he counted tonight's money and I washed the floor, to get most of the dirt off.

"Anne, just leave it. We'll finish up tomorrow."

I thanked him and left with Pete, ready to help him, but he seemed to have sobered up during those fifteen minutes. It was pitch black outside. The moon was beautiful.

"Sorry 'bout all that."

"No problem. I've seen much worse at the pub. You said that Rebecca was having strange reactions?"

"It's been getting hard to recognize her. She disappears all night sometimes. She barely eats anymore. I thought that going out with that French guy would help her, but it hasn't."

The French guy. He was talking about Mathieu. He also disappeared for nights on end. Unless they were together then?

"You're French too, I can tell by your accent. I saw you go outside at night, walking around the little lake behind our place. You're nuts to do that in the middle of the night! You have to be careful; that house brings misfortune. My mom knew Elizabeth Melville and her daughter well. She had a hard life, tortured by both the living and the dead."

My heart started beating harder—now I was the one who needed support, not Pete. He looked fine now. I didn't say anything, listening to his revelations, dumbfounded.

"My mom told me lots of creepy stuff about this house. But you must know all that. Everyone here knows what took place at Lochan Wynd."

Alex had revealed the secret of Elizabeth's mom's terrible death to me. Maybe there were other mysteries here too? We'd arrived and Pete didn't tell me anything else.

"You want to come up for one more? I've got good Scottish music."

I was curious to visit this house and see Rebecca's paintings. And with a little luck, Pete would fill me in with more information about Lochan Wynd, so I accepted.

He opened the door and nearly tripped on the step. He put his finger to his lips.

"Shhhh... My father and sister must be sleeping, we don't want to wake them up."

I wasn't the one making the most noise here. I followed him. He turned on the lights. A traditional living room. I immediately noticed a picture of a young lady next to the TV.

"Is that a portrait of your mother?

"It is. She was beautiful, wasn't she?"

I nodded. The way she died was really strange. Why on earth walk right next to a cliff when the path leading to the beach was just a few steps away? And how could she have fallen right in the middle of the afternoon? Once again, the sea played its part.

Pete came back with two bottles of beer.

"Sorry, there's nothing to eat, my dad emptied out everything."

"He must find it hard."

"For sure. He thinks it's his fault. Had he been with her that day, it wouldn't have happened. And he's worried about Rebecca."

"How come?"

"Because of the Lochan Wynd curse."

The Lochan Wynd curse? From a secret, it turned into a curse...

"You're kidding, aren't you? You know Halloween is over, no need to try to scare me."

"Come here, I'll show you something."

I had a knot in my stomach, with the feeling that I'd finally know what these revelations were. We tiptoed up the stairs. Each step we took made the stairs squeak, but that didn't seem to stop the continuous snoring from his father, I presumed. In the dark, we carefully found our way and I heard him slowly open a door.

"See, she's not here tonight either."

We went in and he turned on the light. It was Rebecca's room. She had a very feminine decoration in it, with a satin bedspread, thick colorful drapes, and an antique vanity full of makeup and creams without forgetting her many hairbrushes. There was an easel covered with a sheet in the room, and Pete took it off.

"This is what she's painting. My sister is gifted in art. But her stuff freaks me out."

There were several superimposed paintings on it. The first one was the Scottish seaside, with cliffs separating the rough sea on one side from the moors on the other. Perhaps this was in memory of her mother? It seemed normal to me to express the way you suffer when a loved one passes. It was a beautiful painting, with contrasted colors and emotions. I looked at the next one. It was easy to recognize the lake and woods behind our house.

"The Witch Lake."

I turned my eyes to Pete, astonished.

"The *Witch* Lake?"

"Yup. That's what people here call it. They say that women went there to perform witchcraft. You don't see anything weird on these paintings? Take a close look here, there's a white silhouette in the water. And on the other one, she drew faces with their eyes closed in the sea."

I only noticed this when he pointed it out to me. That lake. First Elizabeth's mom who was drowned there, and now a venue for witchcraft. Maybe this explained that: the feelings of hallucinations that I had when I was there, the guys who advised me not to go down by the lake, all of Tom's warnings when I first came. I shivered.

"Today someone talked to me about The Witches' Mountain. Is that linked to the lake here in Lochan Wynd?"

"Not really. But that's where they burned the so-called witches back then, didn't they?"

I nodded and Pete continued to comment on other paintings.

"Flames where you can see faces. The face of a man who's screaming. And an inert silhouette in each painting. Dead people. Fuck, ever since my mom died, Rebecca only draws dead people."

He sighed and took another sip of his beer. I didn't know what to say here. Just looking at these pictures I never would have seen that underlying theme. My head started to pound, and I was dizzy. I had to sit down. My migraines had showed up again. And all this information was getting mixed up in my head. Was it because I was exhausted, not sleeping enough, I had no idea but I couldn't make head nor tail of this. Rebecca was painting dead people's faces? Was she crazy or what? When I first met her, I was convinced she was peculiar, but not to this point. And all those "protections" she'd put in place for Mathieu: the knife under the pillow, those strange signs she'd painted in his room. Besides, I'd seen her go to the lake: was it to do witchcraft there?

Pete went on explaining.

"At first my dad and I didn't realize what was going on with Rebecca. She carried on painting and we thought it was cool. After that though, things started to go downhill, she decided to eat only twice a week and skipped all the other meals. She said it was for a healthier life. And now she leaves for days on end and when she comes back, she's got an absent expression in her eyes. One evening when she wasn't in her room, I saw her paintings and right away I felt that something wasn't right."

"I certainly understand your concern. Did either of you talk to her?"

"To Rebecca? She said everything's fine, but that's a bunch of bullshit. Something really strange happened when my mother died. She'd written a will."

"Had she? But she was so young."

"She was. But apparently, she'd believed that something bad would happen to her for a long time. So anyway, when she died, they opened the will: my mom had left things for each of us. And my sister inherited this old album, she's always hidden it. But I found it one day."

He pulled an old leather notebook out of one of the drawers in the desk and handed it to me.

"Take a look. You'll understand why this freaks me out."

I carefully took the notebook from him. There was a sign that I recognized right away on the cover: the same one as the one on the ceiling in my old room. The circle holding three ovals together.

"What does this sign mean?"

"I don't know. But nothing good in my opinion."

I opened it up. On the first page an old quote in calligraphy handwriting.

"It is said that all descendants of these women will become insane or die after dawn."

It was above portraits of women with a first name and a date. The first one was dated 1754. I turned the pages quickly. Black and white photos gradually replaced the drawings. Some were just portraits of faces, others were wider, sometimes with background scenery. There were only women, and the dates were in chronological order. Most of them were wearing old-fashioned clothes—long black dresses with white collars. They were pictured as they had been when living, in front of their house, sitting against a tree, or by the lake. I put the notebook back down, upset.

"Have a look at the last page, there's a portrait of my mother. Weird, isn't it? Rebecca must have drawn it."

He pointed at a sketch that looked like the photo I'd seen in the living room, with Lauren written as her first name.

"This is what your mother willed to Rebecca? How come? Who are all these ladies?"

"Our ancestors."

We remained silent fort a short time before Pete started to explain this.

"All these women are from the same branch and Rebecca and I are their descendants. I don't know who began this book so no one would forget those who died, but I guess it's been passed on from generation to generation, from mother to

177

daughter or sister to sister. And what's really crazy is that there are no men in it. So at the beginning I thought it was like a family tree, not your regular one, but just for women. But one night when my dad had too much to drink, I understood that his delusions were based on reality. He couldn't stop: they should have moved, he was so sorry he hadn't taken her seriously, now he understood what she wanted to say, crap like that. At the beginning I believed he was blaming himself for my mom's death. But little by little, thinking back on what he'd said over time, I realized that it was based on the truth. My mother knew she'd perish young and my dad couldn't do anything to save her. She handled it alone for years, but one day she must have been scared and she shared all that with my father, who thought it was pure bullshit. Because he just couldn't believe what she had told him: this family had been cursed for generations on. All the women either went insane or died prematurely. My mother was persuaded that the same thing would happen to her, so she took the precaution of giving this book to Rebecca in her will. And now she's one of them too. My father couldn't do anything."

Pete had never spoken this long to me, I had the impression that it was another Pete, not just the tattooed guy I thought I knew. In just one evening, I got to know him. The image that I had of him in the beginning, someone superficial and careless was completely false. He was worried and he had to share his concerns with someone. Why me, though? I had no idea. Perhaps because I'd listened to him in the pub. Or because I was a woman. This story was incredible and hard to believe, but nonetheless, the proof was there. I understood his mother's pain in keeping this secret for herself and being rejected when she wanted to share it, I understood his father's guilt when he couldn't prevent what his wife was dreading.

"So now Rebecca's got the book," Pete continued. "Things don't look good. How can I prevent anything? She pretends it's nothing... My dad is useless, languishing in his living room, drinking. For the portraits in the book, of course, I didn't recognize everyone, but there was my grandma on my mother's side, who ended up crazy, and the two sisters, Emily and Margaret, one who also went crazy and the other one who drowned in Lochan Wynd Lake. My mom told me about that when I was little so I would never go near the lake."

"Wait a minute, you mean that Margaret drowned in the lake? Like Elizabeth's mom did?"

"Margaret *was* Elizabeth's mom."

Oh, so that meant that the letter I'd found in the book had been written by her. That explained everything.

"*Forgive me...*" her last words before she drowned herself. But then how could Margaret also be in the album? Was she one of Rebecca's ancestors?

"So you're a part of Elizabeth's family then?"

"Well, extended family. Emily, my grandma's grandma, was Margaret's sister."

A sharp pain shot through my body, like an electrical shock, and I had to close my eyes for a second. Rebecca was one of Alex's distant cousins. He hadn't told me that! Margaret was

Elizabeth's mom. And Emily, her sister, had gone mad. I was dazed by all these revelations. Was Alex's mother endangered too then? And Elizabeth, who was now 95, did she escape all of this? It must have been hard for Rebecca. Perhaps that explained why she went out at night? Did Mathieu know all this?

"Did you ask Elizabeth for any advice? At her age, the curse seems to have missed her. You should talk about this, ask her."

"Alex told me that she's pretty senile. It's too late now."

"Did Rebecca say anything about this?"

"Nothing at all. I don't know who to talk to. Rebecca's ignoring me, my dad's drunk all the time..."

He paused and finished his beer. I was no longer thirsty.

"Alex told me about you. I know what happened," he finally let out.

Was he talking about the episode in the bathroom? Or the knife? He continued before I could ask him.

"You live in the house, you interact with her. I thought maybe you could help me."

I didn't know what to say. Help him? But how? I just learned about all of this. And what role was the house playing in it?

"Pete, if that can help, I can tell you that I dreamed about your sister once. And in my dream, there were other women at the lake. And I saw her go out once in the middle of the night and I think she was going there too. Did you know that? What do you think she could have been doing there? Secret meetings? Black magic with so-called witches?"

"Witches my ass, they don't exist! What would she be doing at the lake; she's got a phobia of water!"

"You're sure about that?"

"Totally. She almost drowned when she was little. Anne, you have to find a solution to get my sister out of this mess. She likes you."

Why me though? I had no idea why Pete believed I could help her. I wasn't sure that Rebecca liked me, quite the opposite actually as she'd encouraged me to go down to the lake, which led to what happened in the bathroom. Se nearly got me kicked out of the house with her knife... And the way she looked at me.

"I really don't think she likes me. I've got the impression that she considers me an obstacle between her and Mathieu."

"You're wrong."

I walked to the easel and he showed me another painting.

It looked like a scene from the apocalypse. A forest burning and a lake—one that I knew only too well—with red reflections from the fire. And above it, my face, mixed in with pink clouds, surrounded by candles and flowers, floating in a halo of light.

"You're in several of them. She knew that you would bring her luck. Now it's up to you: will you be the one she's been waiting for? Anne, you're our only hope."

— CHAPTER ELEVEN —

I spent the whole night dwelling on what Pete had revealed to me. In Mathieu's room, I went to and fro, from my bed, my pack of cigarettes, to the window overlooking Rebecca's place. Everyone else was sleeping or being quiet behind their closed doors, and I didn't want to stay in the living room or kitchen. I had checked the strange symbol above the bed, and it was the same as the one in the album with the portraits of those women. This just wasn't possible. This curse, it perhaps was just a few unfortunate coincidences and superstitions. Pete must have been pulling my leg here!

But the proof was there, in Rebecca's room: her paintings, her drawings of myself, and the notebook that was handed down generation after generation... How could she ever believe that I would be a hope for her? Because I'd slept in the room overlooking the lake? How could I help her? This was crazy, it was hard for me to remain lucid myself. And why didn't she say anything to me? Why had Pete waited so long if his sister was in mortal danger?

And this never-ending headache was killing me. I'd popped a pill when I returned, but it hadn't kicked in yet. The pain was now lodged in my right temple, beating deafeningly, in rhythm with my heart.

They'd said that the women would either go crazy or die, something like that was written. *"After dawn."* Why after dawn? I looked up the definition of dawn in the dictionary.

"Light appearing at the horizon just before sunrise; moment corresponding to the beginning of a day."

Dawn, the morning, just before sunrise. What morning? After what night? Because dawn was also the end of the night. Was it a symbol? The dawn of life? But then how could anyone define the dawn of life and when? There was another definition.

"Beginning of something, of an era."

Maybe this sentence meant the moment right before a change, or becoming aware of something? Going from one stage of life to another? I really had no idea how that could define when something would happen to Rebecca. How much time did I have if I wanted to help her? And the third definition was *"Dawn-Aurora,* also named Anthocharis cardamines or Orange Tip Butterfly: white butterfly with orange-spotted wings." So dawn could also be a butterfly that was common in the woods, one that laid its eggs on a plant called Cardamine, but that made even less sense.

Perhaps Alex was trying to protect me when he wanted me to leave the house. Did he know that his cousin was endangered?

Had he heard about the curse? I doubted it, I was sure that if he had, Pete and he would have done everything they could to prevent it.

I grabbed the old book on St Andrews, the one by John Bower, where I'd found Margaret's message on a sheet of paper. I read it again. Elizabeth's mother had written this in 1914, before committing suicide.

"I'm dying because I bother
Those around me
Those people without parsimony
Do the same to me!
I hate the wind and the rain;
I hate the heat and the cold;
I therefore abandon my life
Without regrets and without fear. Please forgive me."

Someone crazy wouldn't write words like that. Alex had nonetheless told me that after her husband died, she went insane, talking to herself and looking out the window for hours on end. But someone crazy wouldn't have premeditated her suicide nor left a poem so she would have been forgiven. And why did she want to kill herself? The text insinuated that those around her wore her down. Those in the village? She'd locked Elizabeth in her room, probably to protect her, but from whom?

I had so many questions about this house and what had happened here.

It was 4:22 a.m. I was exhausted but knew that as soon as I'd closed my eyes, I wouldn't be able to sleep. I looked at the calendar: December 15th. I'd be returning home in a few days. I still hadn't told anyone. Mathieu was aware of it, but would he remember? I hardly ever saw him now. I felt like my friends who used to be so close to me had now abandoned me. I almost wanted to live without even letting them know. Leaving everything. Anyway, for them I was nothing at all. They didn't understand what I was enduring. On the other hand, Guillaume, my love, my fiancé, was waiting for me. I'd have to call him so he'd come pick me up at the airport in Marseille, unless I wished to surprise him. I smiled at the idea. I'd give him a call when I was back in France, he wouldn't be expecting anything! Then it occurred to me that I hadn't thought about Lara for weeks. Incredible! I was ready then to go back to my former life. It seemed so far away. Going back to Guillaume, to his hands, his warmth.

I could even start packing now. I tiptoed into my former room, the one facing the lake. Mathieu wasn't there and hadn't been back for days. I wondered where he was and was sure that he wouldn't appreciate the idea that I kept on going into this room. But as he wasn't there to stop me...

My luggage was still under the bed, eager to travel back to France. It was strange to look at this huge bag, like an object from another era. There were also dust bunnies, a pen, and other souvenirs of my stay here. I could see William, Alex and

Mathieu smiling at me, I could feel the wind on the pier at the little port, I could remember the evenings we spent at the pub, walking through the town, shopping at Tesco. The damp beach, like a tongue, the rain that soaked me, the lake. All of this just by looking under the bed, I'd never forget any of it.

I got most of my stuff out of the room and packed it. Then I turned off the light and waited, sitting on the bed. There were presences in this room, I knew it, and they weren't hallucinations. I'd seen them and heard them before. I mentally implored them.

"Come on, show yourselves! Don't be scared. Tell me everything."

I waited; eyes closed. Maybe they'd explain to me what I wanted about Elizabeth, about her mother, about the lake. I wasn't afraid of the shadows, of what could happen. I just wanted to know. I wanted them to speak to me.

"Tell me who you are. Tell me how I can help."

Little by little, the silence was less complete. A slight whirr, like a hummingbird's wings, could be heard. Indistinct and agitated shapes began to appear. They moved as soon as I looked at them. Shadows whispered, but I didn't understand a word. They all spoke at the same time in an unintelligible language. They flitted around me. I held my breath so I could concentrate. I slowly made out the forms of the shapes. I could see blurred faces, running together in the frenzy of their whispers, then more and more precise details, eyes, hands... These whirring sounds, now like fallen leaves in the wind, were becoming louder.

There were people, so many people, in this room. They were everywhere, never stopping, and it was hard for me to observe them. I nonetheless could distinguish some of them. The face of a man with his eyes close together, one I immediately recognized, and a strong whiff of something burning. I pronounced his name out loud, to confirm who it was.

"Patrick Hamilton?"

It was shaped like a suspended face in front of me, without answering, as if it were examining me, then another shadow zipped in front of it, floating in the air. Several entities seemed to introduce themselves to me, nearly fighting, both men and women. With each appearance, the room reacted differently, in symbiosis with each entity: an odor of moist earth, water running on walls, the room suddenly turning red, and I could hear a rustling. Then there was another face with the sound of a hot fire. It must have been another of the martyrs in St Andrews. In my dream, they had asked me to help them. Was this what they really wanted?

"Tell me what you want. Tell me what to do."

The frenzy of the shadows slowly calmed down and I could see immaterial expressions: pain, worry, anger. What they were feeling. They came together to create an image and I recognized Lochan Wynd Lake. There were people with torches, then the image faded away and was replaced by another, this time North Street, and I could clearly spot John Forrest's house.

"I don't understand. What am I supposed to do?"

Their background noise didn't make any sense, it was confused. I felt things though. They suffered pain, perhaps they were still suffering. They were worried and anxious about something or someone. But what? Once again, this damn lake was in the heart of it. And what about Forrest's house? This vision reassured me that my drawing was right. What were they trying to show me?

All these questions. At the end of the day, did it mean anything?

I spent most of the night thinking about that, immobile, rocked by their nearly inaudible whispers, without being aware of time.

— CHAPTER TWELVE —

I walked into town a bit before dawn. It was very early in the morning. On this chilly December morning, my eyes took in what they soon would no longer be able to.

I was going to miss St Andrews. I now knew the city so well that I'd made myself a mental map, a virtual tour printed forever in my head that would allow me to visit whenever I wanted to. I'd never forget this little city, its winding roads, its pubs, its monuments.

Morning had not yet broken, it was drizzling, and I was happy. I felt like I belonged here. I knew I'd changed. I now paid attention to things when I was out and about. Reflections, shadows, Mother Nature, movements of plants in the wind. I listened to birds and the hum of their wings. I felt the moistness of the earth, the softness of the moss on the stones. I observed crows eating away at carcasses, rabbits curled up sleeping or on the other hand, fleeing as soon as I approached, magpies swallowing worms they'd just pulled out. I looked at people in the streets, their smiles, their shoes, their habits. I recalled all the time I'd spent in "Bonnie Scotland". I took a deep breath. The world was so beautiful. Seeing everything, learning everything! My spirit had opened itself up here.

I'd liked wandering around. Alone in the countryside, amongst smells of the earth and the bright yellow flowers waving in the breeze. Walking down little paths, going from here to there, without a precise route. Trying to reach a small wall I'd seen from afar, climbing up a hill to admire the view, lying on the ground to look at the sky. Taking advantage of this landscape that was so peaceful and calm.

The town had its own fragrance, one I was unable to define. The way Scotland smelled. The Scores, Tesco, The Drinking Bastards Pub, all these places I'd been to and that had changed me, where I'd forgotten my misfortune. I'd bought fish & chips, I'd gone to the movies, I'd played pool at the pub, with its scent of wax and beer. Time had gone by so quickly. I'd been in town—how many times already?—to the seaside, in the wind, in front of so many huge waves. St Andrews was a beautiful city, with its old buildings, though they remained young, because of all the students. St Andrews was the sun and rain at the same time, wind and clouds. St Andrews was a microcosm of the universe.

The town was still sleeping. Everything was calm under the street lights. My feet had taken me to this place that I loved, the pier in the old port. The sea was rocking slowly, like a large and heavy sheet, and I could smell its freshness.

I stayed there for a while, contemplating this huge body of

water. I never wanted to forget this place. I could hear the sweet sound of waves lapping and the fishermen's boats lightly tapping against the wharf in the port. The air smelled like algae and fish. I remembered what Mr. Forrest had told me: back in the olden days, the wharf was made from wood, before being rebuilt using stones from the castle. I also imaged the shipwrecked boat and John Honey swimming to save its passengers.

I walked near the cathedral. I could almost see a white silhouette in the tower and smiled, thinking of Prior Robert de Montrose. So many legends here...

I reached Mr. Forrest's house. It was much too early. I sat down on the sidewalk across the street and waited till daybreak. He had had a strange reaction when I spoke about Lochan Wynd, like he was lost in his thoughts. I was sure he knew things, maybe even things about the house. I had to talk to him again. Should I go for broke and present my diagrams to him so he'd explain why the point connecting where those martyrs died led to his house? I was afraid he'd react like William and tell me I was ridiculous.

When was it going to get light out? At this time of day no one was yet walking in the streets and the town was completely still. My eyes were suddenly attracted to a movement. A bit farther down the street, on the left side of Mr. Forrest's house, the wall seemed to be shivering. I got up, rubbing my eyes. I hadn't slept a wink that night. My eyes were heavy and it felt like my head was floating in thick clouds. Yet, this was how I'd been for ages and I was used to it. There was a well whose surface had been blocked off by a metallic grid there. I waited a bit but didn't perceive anything else. Was my fatigue playing tricks on me?

Then I saw them. Barely noticeable little shadows, like tiny clouds without any consistency, were flittering discreetly above the well and floating next to the wall. Like they'd come out of that well. Some of them seemed to be carrying torches. Was this even possible? Seeing things wasn't normal. I was afraid.

I looked around, but no one was out. I carefully approached and heard a minute whirring, like feathers rubbing together. It seemed like these shadows were watching me.

They suddenly began moving, inviting me to follow. They ran along the facades of the houses, on the stones, avoiding the windows and doors. Where were they going? What did they want to show me? I followed them, walking at a quick pace, so I wouldn't lose them. They flew down North Street towards the west, towards the city center. Why didn't they go to the opposite side, towards the cathedral, where the cemetery was? The shadows pushed against one another, intertwining, then moving away, leaving a gap between the first and last ones. They turned onto College Street, continued down Market Street and St Mary's Place. The agitated crowd was going faster and faster, leaping from one road to another, in a delicate confusion. I had to start running to catch up with them and follow them to Hepburn Gardens. I could see their lights bobbing far in front of me, like fireflies. Not a light on in the houses we passed. I'd have to run faster if I didn't want to lose them.

"Wait!"

They must not have heard me though and the shadows veered to the right towards St Leonards Road. I turned there too. Where were we going? I was really out of breath, running wasn't a strong point for me, they'd have to slow down. I could still make out their lights and kept following them. I'd finally know what they wanted. In one ultimate effort, as I was familiar with this neighborhood, I began a final sprint: we were nearing Lochan Wynd and the strange shadows were at the end of the path leading to the lake. The sun chose that very moment to come up, dawn had broken. Just a couple of feet and I'd be at the curve they'd taken.

I ground to a halt, huffing and puffing, looking for a movement, a light. Nothing. They'd disappeared without a trace. Evaporated! All I could see was the lake, in the morning sun, surrounded by huge trees. What a disappointment! Why had they led me here? Right back to where I'd started off?

The lake was strangely silent. Not one bird was singing and even the wind had fallen. I felt like I was being watched. As usual, there was no one, no one but these impressive trees with their quivering bark. I was shivering with cold now and didn't want to stay.

I slowly walked back up to North Street, a bit disappointed, but more and more curious. Why had these shadows revealed themselves to me and then abandoned me just after? I had been attentive and had come after the vision they'd sent to me. Who were they? They must have been ghosts of the martyrs; I was sure I'd recognized Hamilton. Who were the others? There were so many of them. I'd have to pay more attention, try to know them and recognize them.

I bravely rang Mr. Forrest's doorbell. No answer. I had to talk to him, even if it was early.

I rang the bell again, and as there still was no answer, I turned the doorknob on the blue door and ventured in.

"Mr. Forrest?"

I heard a weak "aye" that seemed to come from upstairs.

"It's Anne. Are you upstairs? I'm sorry I came so early."

"Come on up."

I started up the stairs. His voice seemed so weak. Maybe I'd woken him up? I thought old people always got up early.

He was in his room, in bed, hooked to an artificial respirator. I pulled up a chair and sat down next to him. I was uncomfortable seeing him in this position. I remembered that he seemed to have trouble breathing the first time I'd seen him, but I never would have imagined he needed all these wires and oxygen. The machine breathed regularly.

"Hello Mr. Forrest. I hope I'm not bothering you."

"Let me unplug this."

He had a nose mask with a harness to hold it on but it didn't cover his mouth. He took it off and carefully shut the respirator down.

"I didn't know that you needed artificial respiration."

"This is just a mechanical device, but I dinnae use it durin' the day, just at night."

He stopped talking to get his breath back. Now he had to force his lungs to breathe by themselves again. As his chest went up and back down, I heard a distant sound, almost a death rattle, like little stones moving on the bottom of a stream in an unending river.

"I can come back later if you want."

He shook his head and made a gesture with his hand, telling me this idea was completely absurd. But I was sure he was annoyed to be seen like this. He looked as if he hadn't shaved for days, his chin was covered in stubble and his hair was a mess.

"I'm ready, Lass, I'm ready."

He ran his fingers through his hair, pushing it back, as if he had read my thoughts.

"We'll stay here if it's all richt fur ye. Mr. Barlett is really lucky to have enthusiastic students like ye in his class."

I just smiled so I wouldn't contradict him.

"Are ye makin' progress in yer dissertation in History? What was it about again?"

"You know, it's pretty vast. I've been working for the last few months on the places where those martyrs died. Drawing on all the information you've given me and my research, little by little, I was able to make this map. So, as you can see, each of the martyr's funeral pyres was here."

And my heart pounding, I showed him my diagram. I explained my process to him, the shape of the cross, the epicenter of these lines and especially this street and his house in particular.

He asked me to hand him his glasses on his bedside table.

"I think your house is special, it's smack in the middle of these events. You might think this is strange, but I've spent months studying this. Look here, the lines trace the ruins of St Mary on the Rocks, that's a sign, isn't it? And your house is right in the middle."

"I see, I see."

He seemed a bit dumbfounded by my presentations, looking at them without saying anything. Was he wide awake at least? He finally answered after a few interminable minutes.

"Astonishin' work, Lass, very exact an' well documented."

He paused briefly to catch his breath.

"I must admit though, I dinnae see how ye could have reached those conclusions. What link does my house have with all this?"

"I was hoping you could tell me. Did you ever notice anything special? Think about it."

"Nae, never. I've stayed here fur over forty years, an' this is a completely normal house, a nice one, with a view o' the St Andrews Bay an' the ruins o' the castle."

I glanced over at him. His face still held traces of the respiratory mask he'd worn all night. His chest was rising quickly, as if he had run a sprint and was out of breath, and his tired eyes seemed to have lost their sparkle.

"The well that's in the road, right next to your house, is it yours?"

"Nae just mine, it's a shared well an' erstwhile people came here fur their drinkin' water."

Should I tell him about their shadows I saw coming out of that well? He'd think I was nuts.

I didn't want to insist, I still had lots of things to ask him but didn't want to scare him away. Last time he'd told me that he had never done any extensive research on the origins of his house. Was it really ancient, as I'd thought? Had one of the martyrs lived here? I'd have to make my own inquiries; it was my duty.

"Thank you, Mr. Forrest. I also brought this, I thought you might be able to help me here."

I showed him that strange sign that was both on the ceiling of Mathieu's room, preventing me from sleeping, and on Rebecca's book, the one that had all the pictures of those women. This time he was much more loquacious.

"This is a well-known Celt symbol, called a Triquetra. It has its origins with the number three, representin' nae only the divine trinity, Father, Son, an' Holy Ghost, but also the cycle o' life: birth, life an' death, or the three main elements, water, air an' fire."

He stopped, closing his eyes, calming the muffled rumbling coming from his chest.

"The three loops are united by a circle, symbolizin' eternity. Fur witches though, the Triquetra invokes feminine cycles: the young lady, the mother an' finally the old lady. Here the circle symbolizes fertility an' protects the person wearin' it from evil."

I jumped when I heard the word "witch." So for witches then, it was a good sign. That seemed to work. I was sure that Rebecca had close links with witchcraft. All these weird things that happened because of her. Those protections that she'd put in Mathieu's room. The knife! She must have wanted to protect me too then. But from what? I wasn't one of the descendants targeted by the curse, she was the one who was in danger! I had to see Mathieu. He knew that Rebecca was trying to keep him safe, maybe he also knew what she was trying to protect him from. But he had been the invisible man for the past few days.

I encouraged M. Forrest to go on.

"Last time you told me about Witches' Mountain. Can you tell me more? And about Lochan Wynd Lake?"

"I dinnae like the term 'witch,' because it's pejorative. There's nae a monument fur the 'witches' in St Andrews, like the martyrs, although they suffered just as much. Those so-called witches often ended up bein' hanged or sentenced to burn to death either in Market Cross or on Witches' Mountain. Before that, they had to undergo unbearable torture: they were thrown into Lochan Wynd Lake, with their arms an' legs crossed an' attached. If they sank, they were declared to be innocent an' pulled out with a rope, but if they floated an' survived, it was because o' their witchcraft an' they were immediately burned at the closest stake."

I listened carefully to the old man whose voice broke every once in a while, interrupted by his difficult breathing.

"A load o' terrible things happened at Lochan Wynd Lake. This test had been validated by the king, but there were also more sordid techniques. They were often prevented from sleepin', an' the lack o' sleep led to hallucinations an' strange erroneous confessions. Sometimes they looked fur 'the devil's mark', some place on their bodies where they didnae feel pain or they had a birthmark. Many people were falsely accused o' witchcraft. That was often a method they used to get rid o' someone, like Nic Neville who was burned at the stake in St Andrews fur necromancy, or Agnes Melville, who was publicly humiliated fur witchcraft."

So many terrible things had taken place in Lochan Wynd. It was awful! He started up again.

"Many o' these women simply practiced white magic, healin' people usin' plants an' Mother Nature. What a waste. An' then when everyone had forgotten all o' this, Lochan Wynd Lake became a vacation spot: people bathed there in the 1900s! Will that help ye fur yer thesis, Lassie? Still nae takin' any notes?"

"I don't need to, I remember everything. All this is really

201

interesting. So tell me, you lived in Lochan Wynd. Did you ever hear of anything that was supernatural or strange that happened there?"

"What do ye mean by that? Ye know, to each his own... It's true that this place is known fur sparkin' misfortune. Tragic things took place there an' the inhabitants have never forgotten them. Some o' them even joke that the house at Number 7 is haunted. Strange, right? I can tell y' that I've got fond memories o' Lochan Wynd, where I stayed from 1936 to 1940. It's a bonnie place, a haven o' peace an' beauty, despite its dramatic past."

"You know, I live there and I see what you mean. Can you tell me what really happened? What tragic things are you talking about?"

"Ye're sure ye want to know, Lass? Because once ye do, it'll be hard to forget all this an' livin' in Lochan Wynd will be much more difficult."

He looked at me seriously, like someone who knew things that were exhausting him. I remembered the first night I'd spent in the room overlooking the lake, after Alex had told me about Margaret's tragic fate. I barely closed my eyes that whole night. But I had to know if I wanted to leave this place in peace, to be sure to have accomplished my mission.

"I live at Alexandre's place and I am already aware of how his great-grandmother drowned. You told me about those poor witches. I think I'm ready to hear the rest."

"It's up to ye."

He sat back up in his bed, adjusting the pillows.

"Before we start, could ye give me a glass o' water please?"

"Of course."

I opened the bottle on his bedside table and filled a glass. He drank a few sips, swallowing noisily and unpleasantly, and put the glass back down.

He finally began speaking, looking like someone who was preparing to unveil something serious.

"It all started at the beginnin' o' the 17th century. There was this lassie, Dorothy, who lived alone in St Andrews, but who was really popular. People came to her from miles around fur her talent as a healer. She helped people who couldnae afford doctors: deliverin' babies, concoctin' love potions, preventin' diseases usin' rites o' mixtures o' plants. So Dorothy practiced white magic without earnin' a cent, what she wanted was to help those in need, an' she often didnae ask fur any financial compensation. People would thank her an' give her a chicken, eggs, a sack o' flour, or a ham.

"Dorothy believed in Mother Nature an' tried to live in harmony with her, respectin' each plant or animal. She used natural energy fur her healin' rites.

"Robert an' Harriet Lewis had been married fur three years, but they still didnae have any bairns. As Harriet was afraid that her husband would leave her, she consulted Dorothy, who gave her a potion to take every day. A few months later, Harriet got

203

pregnant, an' was overjoyed. The two women became friends. But Robert was attracted by the mysterious charm Dorothy had. Neglectin' his pregnant wife, he often visited the young lass, even helpin' her pick the medicinal plants she needed. What he really wanted was to take her to bed, which happened. When Harriet found out, all she could think about was vengeance. Dorothy had put a spell on her husband, seducin' him! But what could she do, so far gone? One day, when she went to the market, she saw a poster askin' each inhabitant to denounce anyone suspected of bein' a heretic or a witch. People had already denounced witches in an' around St Andrews. An' Harriet knew what happened to them then. They were either burned at the stake or hung in public an' no one ever spoke o' them again. She thus decided to betray her friend.

"Dorothy had helped at least half o' the population o' the town an' knew most o' the bairns. Yet she was arrested fur witchcraft, no one supported her. So-and-so had heard her say some magical words in front o' his field an' his crops had all died: she'd cast a spell on him. Someone else saw her take part in some nocturnal ritual, recitin' incantations in the forest behind Lochan Wynd Lake. The doctor didnae like what Dorothy did either, as it made him lose customers, an' thus declared that if she knew how to heal without havin' studied, it was because she was a witch an' had to die. Her house was raided an' they found herbs, semi-precious stones, an' even a cat, the Devil himself.

"Dorothy's fate was sealed. She couldnae defend herself. Robert didnae try to help her either. Locked in St Andrews' prison, she was tortured fur days on end, plunged into the icy water in Witches Loch, nearly starved to death, up until she admitted things she'd never done. She was thrown into the deepest part o' Lochan Wynd Loch, with stones attached, to atone fur her sins an' purify herself.

"When they finally wanted to remove her body from the loch, it had disappeared. Her executioners crossed themselves an' went back home.

"From that day on, many tragic events began to take place. All those who'd taken part in Dorothy's execution perished in bizarre circumstances. The doctor died from an acute infection. Others who'd accused her passed away from epidemics, sudden deaths, or strange accidents. Some o' her executors drowned, either by fallin' into Lochan Wynd Loch or by a shipwreck in the bay. Only the Lewis family wasnae impacted. Even if Harriet's bairn was born deaf-mute an' simple-minded."

The old man stopped once again, raising the glass to his lips to moisten them, before gulping down what was left. I saw that he was sweating. He seemed to be exhausted by this; I was fascinated. I had the impression that, as I was gathering the scattered pieces of my discoveries, new connections were linking my neurons together. John continued to speak, gazing into space.

"There were soon rumors that Dorothy had placed a curse on people. When she unfairly died, she cited all the others who had uselessly suffered (like herself) or had been persecuted, so that they would haunt the livin': the witches tortured at the loch, the Protestant martyrs. An' all the others. The loch was now inhabited by an underground power. Bairns who dipped their feet in the loch saw hands come out, pullin' them down to the bottom. Soon it was forbidden to go to the loch. Lassie, I'm sure that ye know that a loch is a gateway between worlds. Lochan Wynd had become the eye o' the earth, allowin' the underground inhabitants to see the livin'. An' haunt them.

"The year after Dorothy died, several hundred people also died without any plausible explanations, which o' course was blamed on the Lochan Wynd curse. They dropped like flies. Spontaneous combustion right in the street, possessions, an' oh so many drownin's in the loch. The little woods behind the loch fascinated people, attractin' them despite the fact it was now prohibited, an' in the mornin' there were often bodies floatin' on its surface. Then this faded away, there were fewer an' fewer cases. Witch hunts became a thin' o' the past an' people were no longer tortured without due cause. The curse was forgotten, St Andrews attracted tourists fur its golf course, the loch became just an ordinary loch, an' in 1900, like I said before, people went swimmin' there an' nothin' happened to them."

He paused again. His features had hardened, his wrinkles had become deeper, it was as if he was suddenly ten years older.

"So I told ye that the Lewis family wasnae impacted. That may seem strange to ye. It was just seemin'ly so. Dorothy had cursed all o' Harriet an' Robert's descendants. Fur generations, all feminine members o' this family either went crazy or died prematurely. Harriet's daughter was mentally handicapped. She wasnae the only one. All o' the couple's other bairns went insane.

206

"Ghosts unrelentin'ly haunted the family. The Lewis family had to endure many frightenin' nights to atone fur their betrayal o' their friend. They constantly lived with exhaustin' paranormal phenomena: they heard people screamin', water ran from the inner walls o' their house, objects kept on disappearin'. They lived with dead people, an' some o' them were family members."

He paused once again. The curse that the Lewis family suffered from seemed strangely like the one Pete had told me about. Could Rebecca be one of Harriet's descendants? And Elizabeth's mom, who drowned in the lake? Was it an accident or because of Dorothy's curse? John now had his eyes closed. His face seemed too heavy to support, his eyelids were sunken in, his lips were nearly blue. I touched his shoulder.

"Mr. Forrest?"

No answer.

"Mr. Forrest?"

I pushed his shoulder lightly, before shaking him. He didn't budge. I was terrified. What should I do? Did he just die on me?

I looked at the glass on the table, filled it with water and threw the content of it on his face.

He had a spasm and coughed.

"What are ye doin' Lass?" he mumbled.

"Excuse me, for a moment I thought..."

"What? Just look, my sheets are all wet. Bring me a towel

now."

Colors were coming back in his face, he was alive. He pointed to the bathroom and I brought him a towel.

"Tell me Mr. Forrest, how do you know all that?"

"I did some research too, I must admit. But most o' this I learned from Elizabeth, who told me this when I stayed in Lochan Wynd."

"Can you tell me more about Elizabeth? I would love to meet her!"

A wave of nostalgia swept through his gaze, certainly fond memories of her.

"Bonnie Beth. She was twenty years older than me, but a charmer. All that was before the war."

He ran his hand through his hair, a wry smile on his lips.

"Ye ask an auld man to tell ye about his past... Count me in! Beth was tall, with long brown hair that she always wore in a bun an' dark brown eyes that moved everyone she looked at. She was ferociously independent; she knew what she wanted an' how to get it. She lived alone, but the house was never empty, people were always stoppin' in—her family, her friends. An' she loved to sing. I could hear her from my window, she had a bonnie voice, but as soon as ye complimented her on it, she would stop. She was a simple lassie, ate like a little bird, didnae need much. An' she was always smilin'... Beth, she was one o' a kind."

A normal woman after all, one that never let it known that she was a victim of her family's curse.

"Was she... Was she sad sometimes, like she was tormented by something?"

"She did have her secret world. She never seemed sad when she was with me. The only time I saw her lose her composure was the day when Abigail an' George, her cousin an' her brother, locked themselves in one o' the rooms. She didnae want any doors to be locked, she wanted them to remain open."

Her neurosis about locked doors was that old then.

"Do you still see each other?"

"Nae... When the war was over, I moved here in North Street. War changes everythin' ye know, time goes by, things are different. When I got back, I learned that she had a four-year-old daughter. I never dared see her again... Our story probably just lasted a few months fur her."

You could tell from his voice that he regretted this. He lowered his eyes. Had they been lovers? I glanced at my watch; it was nearly 11:00.

"I have to run, time has flown by! I'll never be able to thank you for all you've done for me. Will Lorna be stopping by today?"

"The nurse will come first, give me that damn shot... It was a pleasure talkin' to ye Lass, ye know that life is sad at my age. I'm all alone. Um, if ye see Elizabeth, tell her that..."

"Yes?"

"Nae, nothin'. Just tell her that I remember her purple flower dress."

"Promise, I'll tell her. Can I bring you anything before I leave?"

"That's fine, thanks, I'll get up now. Goodbye Lass. An' be careful."

"Goodbye Mr. Forrest."

And I ran off to work. My head was buzzing with what I'd just learned. *"Be careful."* Why did he warn me? Because of Lochan Wynd? And why was everyone worried about me, I wasn't in any danger I knew of! Little by little Lochan Wynd's mysteries were being solved. The shadows I'd been seeing were certainly dead people who had suffered and who now claimed the place for themselves, not knowing where to go, waiting for someone at the lake because of what Dorothy had told them. But was Dorothy's curse still active? Mr. Forrest had said that for years now, nothing else had happened. The martyrs I thought I'd seen, all the shadows I'd followed, everyone seemed to be heading to the lake. What role was Rebecca playing here?

I arrived at the pub just in time. It was loaded with forty-something Scots. I would miss that accent so much, I just loved it! I waved to Adam, put on my apron and started taking orders.

"A fish & chips? Got it."

"You're not from here. Where are you from?"

The guy who asked me this had trouble articulating. Once again, betrayed by my French accent.

"France."

"What are you doing here?"

The man said I was lucky to live in France. I suppose that depended on who you were. Maybe he believed it was heaven on earth in France? People in France had problems too. Which I didn't add, of course. I just smiled at him and poured him a beer. The whole pub was resounding with laughter and discussions; people were pushing one another to be served, the restrooms were always full. Quite the atmosphere for noon.

I cleaned the place when we closed. My back and legs were aching. I suddenly felt like an old lady. I finally let Adam know that I'd be going back to France soon and that I'd be quitting. He was a bit disappointed, we got on well together, but I knew deep down that he was relieved to get rid of me and start looking for someone who was more conscientious than I was, because I'd really made a lot of mistakes lately.

"Take care, okay? Get some rest too. A girl of your age shouldn't be tired all the time."

"Thank you, Adam. I'll come over for a drink before leaving."

But I knew I wouldn't. It was strange, I loved the pub, but I felt that once I'd closed its door, I'd never go through it again.

211

I slowly walked back to Lochan Wynd. Thirty-five minutes later, I was sitting in front of the lake.

That lake. We had been so intimate. I liked it, then it scared me. Because of it I'd seen the world differently and that still made me shiver. It was so old. It had seen so much! Yet it remained calm and silent.

I kneeled down on the edge. Was Dorothy down at the bottom? Could she see me, above her, through those trembling waves?

But the lake was impenetrable. Maybe Dorothy finally left for a better place, one where her friends wouldn't betray her.

What could I do for Rebecca? If I understood everything, she was certainly a descendant of the Lewis family, one who was a victim of Dorothy's curse. Pete and Mathieu had told me she was afraid of water, but I knew I'd seen her here. She must have come to the lake to accomplish some witchcraft rituals, or maybe other ones that had protected her from Dorothy up to now.

The key to everything was the lake, I was sure of that. I had to stay.

The afternoon sun warmed my back and felt good. This day had been so long... I fell asleep.

— CHAPTER THIRTEEN —

"**L**ook, you draw a circle, like this. That shelters you in the energy you've called upon. You just have to be patient. They'll come."

Rebecca was with me, in the circle she'd drawn. I was a bit apprehensive, what was going to happen? We were calling upon energy to understand the dead. Was that going to help?

We didn't wait long. We began to hear a gentle whirring, sort of like when leaves rustle in the breeze, before it got closer, then closer again, and it finally surrounded us.

The shadows were blurry, darting here and there but little by little their outline became visible and I saw them clearly. I could even make out faces.

Women, men, and children.

"See, they came to protect me from the curse. Thanks to them, I survive and see the next day. Look closely, some of them are my ancestors. I've gotten to know them. Have you ever met yours? Have you ever hung out with them, talked to them? You know, they help us when we need help."

The shadows scuttled around us. They couldn't stay still. When we wanted to look at their faces, observe them, they turned away from us, as if they were ashamed. But it only took a few seconds to recognize them. All these people... They didn't say a word, but you could read their eyes. They expressed sadness, distress, even pain for some of them. Faces paraded in front of me, blue faces of those who'd drowned, burned faces of the martyrs, faces of women with long hair and strange tattoos, faces of those who'd died of the plague. I saw Nic Neville and William Steward, those who'd been accused of witchcraft. Also James Sharp, the Bishop, Prior Robert de Montrose, Hamilton, Myln, Craw, and Wishart.

I felt a swirl of warm air around us, like a gentle tornado. It was the energy of all these dead people and this energy told us who they were. Just looking at them and I understood.

"Look closely. They're all here, those people who died here, but also elsewhere, your loved ones. They heard you call out to them."

Rebecca took me by the hand.

"Recognize her?"

A beautiful lady with a tired smile floated in front of us. Her hair was full of wet sand. She didn't look away and remained with us for a good while.

"My mother."

I immediately recognized the portrait I'd seen in Pete's living room. It was Lauren, one of the victims of the curse, and she'd thrown herself off the cliff. I turned to Rebecca. She was crying, in silence. She wiped her tears away.

"We can't do anything. Now she lives in another world. But when I come here, I can see her again, as if she had never left us, just for a few minutes."

I didn't know what to say. Was her mother in peace? Was she going to help me save her daughter from the curse?

"I bet she's happy you come and see her. Does she ever talk to you?"

"No. Dead people never do."

Lauren faded away while Rebecca dried her tears.

"Now it's your turn."

"My turn?" She pointed her head towards the person coming to us, the one with her arms crossed. She looked like she was about thirty or so and reminded me of someone... Grandma! She was so beautiful! It was my grandma when she was young, tall, thin, with a bun in her hair. Such smooth skin! And the same eyes. What was she doing there? It was so crazy to see her, as if time had compressed itself so we could live together like two friends.

"Do you think I can talk to her?"

"No, Anne, you can't. She doesn't use words and won't hear

yours."

My heart was pounding, I couldn't prevent a few tears from falling. Grandma was walking towards us, her arms still crossed. But why? She was holding something... In her arms. I held my breath. There was a tiny being... My baby.

I gasped. Grandma was holding my baby in her arms; I knew she was taking care of her and she was safe. But it hurt. I saw her, so little, so fragile, so far from me. Grandma uncrossed her arms, holding the little baby out to me. I could take her! Squeeze Lara against me, see her face again!

I let go of Rebecca's hand and ran to Grandma.

"No, Anne, don't!"

"She's my daughter. I just want to hold her again."

My arms were outstretched towards my baby, my beautiful baby. One more step ... and I was out of the circle. Everything suddenly disappeared. It was like a supernatural force held me down; my head nearly touched the ground and the bitter cold gripped me. I was alone in the night. I'd lost everything.

I stayed there, immobile, for a moment, then got up, shivering. Grass was stuck to my face. I rubbed my cheek before running back home.

As usual, the door wasn't locked and I could hear familiar voices coming from the living room. As if real life was now taking over. I wiped my feet and went in. The guys had invited some friends, Ben, Tom, and Donald. I hadn't seen them for ages.

"Hi everyone!"

Alex had quickly looked away, but Mathieu waved at me and William smiled.

"Hi Frenchie!"

I was freezing so I leaned against the radiator to warm up.

"Would you like a beer? Here," offered Mathieu while handing me a bottle.

I grabbed it and looked at the clock; it was nearly 1:00 in the morning. I didn't believe it. Had I been outside that long? And what happened at the lake? One more crazy dream? What was Rebecca doing there exactly, calling the dead?

Ben was smoking his pipe which stunk, in my opinion, but that still made me want to smoke too. I got my pack of cigarettes out and lit one.

"So, Donald, how's your diary going?"

"Getting bigger every day, each minute."

He still spoke with an accent, but now I could understand him better, that was the advantage of having been here for a couple of months now.

"Hey, Donald, I bet you and Ben know everything there's to know about the legends in St Andrews. About all those poor people." I interjected.

"It's true, there's a legend saying there are ghosts that appear at night to haunt the living. Sometimes girls hear screaming, sometimes they even faint."

"Have you heard Dorothy's story? About Witch's Lake?"

Tom walked up to us.

"Witch's Lake is the one you like Anne. Remember, when you first came? You always walked around by it."

"I know. But how could I have guessed it was called that way? No one told me."

"Lots of dead people in that lake. But now on May 1st, we do what we call the 'May Dip' to ward off bad luck. We all freeze but it's fun! Want to come with us?"

"I'll be gone. I'm leaving St Andrews the day after tomorrow."

"Really? So soon?"

"I know, so soon."

It was hard for me to realize that I was actually going to move away. Like I was afraid to go back home now. Now my life was here, not there. I imagined myself speaking French again. How mundane! I was already nostalgic: I'd miss everything about Scotland. My simple and free life, hand-in-hand with Mother Nature. Back home, I'd pollute with my car, I'd be glued to my cell phone every waking moment, I wouldn't see any wild animals anymore, like these cute rabbits or beautiful birds. I'd be a victim of the work and sleep system. Drive on the right side of the road. Dry, gray and dusty roads. I'd be happy to see my family again, but they would seem so little and vulnerable compared with the immensity of the world. I'd feel as if I had nothing to say to them. Happy to be here, in the warm weather, with the singsong southern accent, hearing the cicadas chirping, basking in the hot sun, smelling the herbs in the scrubland ... but at the same time so lazy. Where was my real life? This was too absurd; I didn't know what path to take.

Mathieu glared at me. Didn't he appreciate that I spoke about the lake after what he'd done to me? What did he think, that I was just going to give up? He should have been there for me when I needed him. I took a sip of beer.

"So, none of you guys have ever heard of what happened to Dorothy? I know more than you, huh? Dorothy, the witch? I've got a good story then."

Alex interrupted me.

"I know it. Dorothy cast spells. No big deal."

If Alex was aware of Dorothy's story, he knew about the curse and the danger it put Rebecca in. How could he not do anything then to help his cousin? Why hadn't he let me know about this?

"Mathieu, do you have any news about Rebecca?" I asked. "You guys seem to spend a lot of time together."

"What do you mean?"

Alex butted into our conversation.

"Hey, are you guys going to take your cars to the Crail strip this weekend?"

"Not me... I wish I could go for a few runs but my Subaru is bein' repaired. Hopefully next week," answered Ben.

"That's a pity."

Then they were silent. I really felt like a fifth wheel here. William was looking elsewhere and Alex was ignoring me. So I turned to Mathieu and carried on.

"You know, because I haven't seen much of you lately. How's she doing?"

Alex got up, cutting me off.

"Let's go. Tom, I'll have a glass of your absinthe that you're hiding in your room. What about hitting the Liquid and Envy Pub in Dundee after?"

"Sounds good. Count me in." answered Tom.

William declined the invitation.

"I can't. No clubbing tonight, I've got an important lecture at nine tomorrow."

"I would have liked to come too, but I can't," explained Mathieu. "I've got papers to correct. Have fun guys."

They got up, and before leaving Tom discreetly whispered in my ear.

"Beware of the shadows at the lake. Alex doesn't like us to talk about it, but at night things go on there. Watch out.

Curiosity killed the cat, as the saying goes."

I was alone in the living room with William and Mathieu. I was exhausted, my head was killing me. William looked at me.

"So, you're leaving soon?"

"Yup, it's almost Christmas and I think you should spend it at home. These couple of months I've been here have really done me a world of good, but now I have to go back to my normal life, at home. What about you? Are you going back home for Christmas too?"

"I'm going to L.A. for two weeks," said William. "It'll be nice to see my friends again. We all booked a room at the Ritz for a New Year's Eve party, we're going to have a blast!"

Back home again then! "When you think of it though, we're still foreigners here," Mathieu observed.

I thought back upon a similar discussion we'd had a while ago, while savoring a cup of hot chocolate.

"Is it just an impression or is Alex completely ignoring me?"

"You have to understand. He's afraid that you'll..."

"That I'll what?"

"That you'll scare everyone. That you'll tarnish his family's reputation. That you'll do strange things. Afraid of all that."

"How come? I'm just trying to understand! No one ever tells me anything and I'm learning incredible stuff about St

Andrews, about the martyrs, about Lochan Wynd, and I want to know it all. I can't just let this go."

"Well, you should. Look what's happened to you Anne. You're fragile, you have to be careful."

"You didn't answer my question about Rebecca. You haven't noticed anything peculiar about her? Did she tell you?"

"What?"

"You know what. Regarding the curse."

"What the hell is this now?"

"Don't try to tell me you don't know what I'm talking about! Pete told me everything. You have to do something! I can't believe Alex is burying his head in the sand."

"I have no idea what you're talking about Anne."

"Rebecca is in danger. Things are happening down at the lake. Dorothy put a curse on the whole family and that's why Alex's great-grandmother drowned. And now Rebecca's next on the list."

"Why Rebecca?"

"She's one of Alex's distant cousins! The curse says that she'll either *'go insane or die right after dawn.'* I saw things, I know you don't believe me, but I swear to you, I'm telling the truth. There are ghosts... Shadows prowling around, some come out of the well on North Street. Things are going on at the lake. I have to understand..."

I was dizzy. I fell onto the sofa and holding my head with my hands. Waves of pain were hammering through my forehead, in rhythm with my heartbeat, and they resonated, over and over and over.

William handed me a glass of soda.

"Here, take this, it'll do you good."

"Thanks."

I gulped it down, but as soon as I'd swallowed, I gagged, and nearly vomited.

Mathieu sat next to me.

"Anne, believe me, Rebecca is fine. I saw her this afternoon. She was shining. She's beautiful, don't worry about her. You have to think of yourself, not her, and rest. You don't look good at all. Are you eating?"

I couldn't remember my least meal, but with this constant fatigue, it was impossible for me to recall everything.

"Mathieu, I want to go back to my room overlooking the lake. I'll be leaving soon, let me enjoy my last days here."

"I'm not so sure that's a good idea. It won't do you any good."

"Please!"

"Anne, just look at yourself! Not now, you're much too vulnerable! Don't you want to rest a bit, be strong for Guillaume?"

Guillaume. I had forgotten him. I couldn't take it any

longer, I was exhausted. Thinking about all that was too much for my brain.

"Okay, I'm going to bed. I really need some sleep. Thank you, guys. It was so nice to get to know you."

"Don't say that, we'll say goodbye at the airport, not before. Goodnight then," said Mathieu.

"Goodnight Anne," said William.

I went upstairs and into the room facing the lake. It was mine after all, and if Mathieu didn't want me to stay here, tough luck. I glanced into the mirror and jumped. Was that me? Did my face really look like that? These sunken cheeks, protruding bones and deep-set eyes with their huge bags, wrinkles and dark circles... My hair was dirty and disheveled. Coffee stains on my teeth. White cheeks and lifeless eyes. An unknown face.

I couldn't take it any longer. To rest, finally! After so much insomnia. I felt that tonight, I'd finally be able to sleep, snuggled tight in Morpheus's arms. I slid into the sheets without getting undressed and was out like a light.

— CHAPTER FOURTEEN —

I suddenly woke up. Loud snores echoed in the room. Mathieu was sitting on a chair next to the bed. Had he seriously looked over me like a mom would for her sick child? I smiled tenderly. He must not have dared wake me up when he found me sleeping and looked after me for a while before falling asleep himself.

It was dark, but halos of light were dancing on the walls. I slowly got up, not to wake him, and tiptoed to the window: I could see bubbles of light floating above the lake. This time I had to see them up close.

I snuck out, put on my coat and walked out into the freezing December Scottish weather. If I did find something this time, I'd have to wake Mathieu up to prove it so he could see for himself that I wasn't crazy. I took the little path leading to the lake, my eyes focused on all these lights in the background. Dawn would soon be breaking. This time there was no hesitation: whatever it was, I had to see it, I had to be there. I wasn't afraid, on the contrary, I was excited, knowing that I'd finally reached my goal.

Yet, something was wrong. I didn't recognize the lake. Of course, in the dark I couldn't make things out well, but beyond that, the landscape was different. It took me a while. But I suddenly understood when observing the halos of light. The forest had disappeared. The dark mass was no longer in the background, the only things left were a few trees standing, each with a luminous halo, around the lake. I was used to going through the woods in the daytime—had I been dreaming or not—and it made me happy, made me feel alive. But there the few trees I could see just sent me an image of death. How could a whole forest disappear?

I slowly approached, intrigued by the vibrating halos. The trees began to move as I went past them. Slowly rocking. But then I realized that they weren't trees, they were men and women. And the halos were torches. Suddenly, as the sky was beginning to get lighter, a whole crowd of ghosts carrying torches rushed up. It was this crowd that had come out of the North Street well, and that I'd tried to follow!

I could see them all, right in front of me. They were still in pain, as they'd left the world of the living violently. I don't think they really wanted vengeance, just that those still living would be able to understand their suffering. Not forget them. They were waiting to ease their pain in the lake, find equanimity again. The water allowed them to regenerate, their torches represented their pain. They'd come from all over, some were martyrs that had come to put out the fire burning inside of them. New ones arrived every day. Sometimes, something prevented them from getting to the lake, and they would wait in the shape of a tree in the forest, to try again the following night, right before dawn. Because that was the time when the lake, a gate between two worlds, opened and offered them redemption.

I realized there never was a forest behind the lake, just a crowd of dead people who were waiting, immobile. The living took them for trees...

The sun began to rise and the lake, just for a few fleeting moments, became agitated, with shadows running here and there so quickly that my eyes couldn't even follow them, breezes that forced me to shut my eyes. The shadows jumped into the water with their torches and disappeared in pulsations of light, as if a superior energy had absorbed them. Some burst into a black cloud, pushed back towards the sky. During these few seconds, I'd lived a thousand years. I felt like I understood everything, the thoughts of each and every ghost, their stories, but also the infinite knowledge of everything in the world.

The sun then rose and the lake became still again. The landscape was now peaceful and looked like it usually did: the little forest was there again, even if, when you watched really closely, each tree was in a different spot now.

I felt like people were looking at me. I knew I was surrounded, surrounded by people waiting to go into the other world. I turned around and faced the house. I loved looking at it from the lake, this omniscient house that had witnessed oh so many things, as if it were the stage manager for a play. I could make out the window in my room and the reflections of the sunrise on the panes. It seemed there was a silhouette there, could it be Mathieu? I waved but he didn't wave back.

I went in, trying to be as quiet as possible, as it still was early. I poured myself a glass of milk in the kitchen while enjoying the calm morning. Strangely, despite what I'd seen, I felt good. In harmony with life. I no longer questioned myself, I now admitted the reality of these inexplicable phenomena. The lake, shadows and torches were all completely normal. I was simply lucky enough to have witnessed this beautiful rite of passage and that was what was important to me: I was no longer ignorant.

I went up to my room, ready to face Mathieu and his good advice, but he wasn't there. Someone was there, standing in front of the window. I could just see the person's back, and gray hair in a bun. I stopped at the doorstep when the person began to speak without turning around.

"It was time for me to come back."

I had never met her, but I knew who it was. Elizabeth.

"Please come in, I didn't just come to admire the view."

Then she laughed wryly and stared at me. I instantaneously thought of how Mr. Forrest had described her: *Beth was tall, with long brown hair that she always wore in a bun and dark brown eyes that moved everyone she looked at.* I didn't know what to say. How did she arrive here? Alex must have gone to pick her up so that I could meet her. But how was she able to stand, Alex had always insinuated that she was in a wheelchair.

228

I came in and shyly sat on the bed.

"Ye know Anne, a window allows ye to be receptive of things surrounding ye. This window is a very special one, I'm sure ye realized that."

"You know who I am?"

"Of course. No one hides anything from me here."

Once again, she chuckled happily. I found her amazing for someone who had just turned 95. She looked 40 years younger!

"Where should I start? Ye werenae chosen by luck lassie. What happened to ye made ye a sensitive person, one who pay attention to things others ignore. This four-leaf clover on yer desk. Ye picked it when ye came. By doing so, it made ye apt to discover the hidden meanin' of things. Somethin' most people cannae do. That means ye have empirical knowledge, perhaps without even bein' aware of it, allowin' ye to contact those no longer livin'. Halloween is the day when the gap between both worlds is the smallest. That's when it's easier fur the dead to visit those still livin'. October 31st is right in the middle of the fall equinox an' the winter solstice. Scots call this day 'Samhain,' an' it's a day of celebration. Maybe y' felt somethin'. I saw ye at the loch this mornin'. So ye know what I'm talkin' about here. Ye can see ghosts or shadows if ye prefer, even when they are the most vulnerable. That's why Rebecca needs ye. Because ye can bridge the gap between both worlds an' resolve conflicts. I came to help ye though because it'll be impossible alone."

"Do you see things too? When you were locked in that

room, did you... Did you see your mother go down to the lake?"

"Aye, I did. I saw her after too, she visits me sometimes in the evenin'."

"It must have been awful for you. Why did she abandon you, because of the curse?"

Elizabeth sat down next to me on the bed.

"It's not that easy. Let me explain."

— CHAPTER FIFTEEN —

"The Lochan Wynd House is a very auld one. I was born in it on December 18, 1899. My Maw gave birth to me right here, in the room facing the road that yer friend Mathieu sleeps in, with the help of the village doctor. My faither, Victor Melville, was twenty-eight at the time an' had married my mither, Margaret, who was seven years younger than him, just the year before.

"My mither an' her sister Emily were maids fur the Paterson family, in North Bell Street. My faither was a fisherman. We all lived together, my brothers George an' Arthur, Aunt Emily an' Uncle Bob, Abigail an' Amber, my cousins, an' Alice, my grandma, here in Lochan Wynd. My mither had six brothers an' sisters, but they'd all left home.

"As a bairn, I thought this life was just perfect! My faither had his own boat docked not too far from the castle, an' he an' my uncle fished together. I remember that I would climb up the cliff as soon as I was big enough, rain or shine, an' we'd play the game of who would recognize his boat first, we also placed bets on how many fish they'd be bringin' back.

"We had a small boat though an' the big ships that carried all sorts of cargo, like coal, potatoes, or salt fur the stores were the ones that really impressed me. These ships had names that made us dream: *Catherine Black*, or *Royal George*. I was fascinated by them, by the sea. Sometimes storms would bring shipwrecks or debris back to the beaches, as the rocks on the seaside were really dangerous. So I mingled with all the gawkers: anyone needin' to be saved, anyone injured? Where was this ship sailin' in from an' what was it carryin'? Sometimes I'd pick up pieces of the boat that washed in, a symbol of elsewhere, an' brin' them back home. I can still remember askin' my faither questions about what he caught that mornin' while he was repairin' his net, like how big the waves were. Did the boat nearly tip when they pulled the net in? He patiently answered all my questions, sometimes tellin' me incredible stories that scared me. He smelled of iodine, I considered him as an explorer.

"He finally decided, to earn more money, to fish on a much larger ship. Fur the past few years Dundee was Scotland's last whaling port. This was a booming activity because of the burlap industry where whale an' seal oils were used as softeners, but also because of urban lightin' that required whale oil, an' there was even whale-oil soap, or creams an' margarine. Even the bones from the whales were used to make corsets!

"The talk of the town was the new generation steamships that fished in the northern seas. My faither dreamed of that ever since the Dundee Antarctic Whaling Expedition was launched in 1892. This would be an opportunity fur him: he'd fish fur eight months, from March to October, but durin' these eight months he would have a guaranteed salary an' then he'd come back home fur the remainder of the year. Uncle Bob was the first person in our family to be interested in fishin' like this, after my poor aunt was interned. He, of course, wasnae happy to have sent her to a facility that cared fur insane people, but she suddenly had gone crazy an' had terrible an' unbearable panic attacks. My mither had taken care of her fur a year, but nothin' changed. When she had attacks like this, the only thing that calmed her down was to put her in cold water. Even the doctors had no idea what to do. She was crazy, that's what they said, an' we finally had to have her interned.

"Anyway, Bob worked in Dundee an' my faither joined him there as they were hiring fifty people fur the *Grande Ourse* crew. This was a whaler that was a hundred an' twenty feet long, twice as big as a whale. Those ships were made from wood, as that allowed them to resist when the ice froze around them. There were two engineers, two firefighters, the skipper, a carpenter, a blacksmith, a cooper, an' a sail repairer, an' all their staff, then the head oarsman, four harpooners, the cook, a doctor, the captain an' his sailors.

"When Bob an' my faither left, we all went to see them off in Dundee. The first year was long an' hard. I imagined my Da as a hero, sailin' through the ice in faraway countries, eatin' whale meat an' meetin' Eskimos. But we all knew his work was dangerous, an' we often heard tales told by other sailors, about how their crewmates died, either washed off the boat or from hunger an' cold. I remember one tale of a guy who survived by eatin' his hat, but he had to have both legs amputated as they froze.

"After my faither left on the whaler, things became more difficult fur my mither. As my aunt had gone crazy an' Alice, my grandma, had passed away, she was alone to raise all of us. I cannae remember how old I was when I realized there were presences in the house, maybe nine or ten. I never saw anythin', but there were doors that slammed shut, unexplainable breezes an' strange noises. An' sometimes these presences were aggressive, especially fur my Maw. At first, I didnae understand why her eyes were red, why she was so tired. I didnae notice anything. Then one day I surprised her when she was sobbin', an' I knew it was because of the ghosts. As a little kid, what could I do, except help her around the house? I didnae know what went on in the world adults lived in.

"When my Da came back that fall, he no longer smelled like iodine, but rather rancid oil. He'd changed. Part of him remained in those cold countries. He explained what he did, how a harpoon worked, how the ship was propelled with a cannon, how he hunted down whales. At first, he was proud to have taken part in the ten tons of bones an' the one thousand five hundred tons of oil collected. It was a long trip. At the beginnin' the crew was motivated an' healthy, but towards the end, exhausted by the months of work, all they could think about was comin' back home, walkin' on the green grass an' baskin' in the sun. There was food fur months onboard, dried meat, conserves, rice, sometime pea soup, an' they also ate seal flippers or fresh salmon that they'd caught. Fur holidays, they even had milk or rum. He also told me about the Eskimos an' Inuit—I remember laughin' when he recounted me how they played soccer together once when it was -30 °C below. When he was back at home, my mither perked up an' was happy—we were an ordinary family once again. But those months flew by too quickly. He would leave again in the spring.

"Years went by, until I turned thirteen. Whale oil street lights were replaced by gas lights. That seemed like an ominous sign to me. How would we ever survive if the whaling industry closed down?

"That fall, my faither didnae come back. Nor my uncle. My mither dressed my brothers, cousins an' myself in our Sunday best an' took us to the Whaling Company. They said that their ship was missin', certainly blocked in the ice in the Baffin Sea, south of Greenland, carried by the polar current towards huge icebergs. Fur the moment they had no signs of life from the crew. It was hard to hope when ye knew how difficult the climate was an' how hard fishin' conditions were. My mither was desperate an' when we saw her like that, we all started cryin'. The Company employee must have pitied us unless he was exasperated by our tears?

'Names?'

'Victor Melville, my husband an' faither of my three bairns, an' Bob Haughs, the faither of these two, my nieces.'

'Here ye go.'

"An' we left with the equivalent of the annual pay of the two men, givin' us enough time to try to turn our lives around. But that didn't replace a faither.

"It perhaps was because I was now older, but it was getting' harder an' harder fur me to see my mither in this strange state. An' my faither's death only made things worse. She often spoke to herself, whisperin' 'Leave me alone!' or whined an' cried. She always looked worried an' often turned around suddenly, as if checkin' that no one was behind her back.

"I wanted to help, but when I asked what was goin' on, she never answered. She never complained an' suffered in silence. I was afraid that she would go crazy like Aunt Emily. As the oldest daughter in the house, I felt like I was the only one to notice that all this wasnae normal, my brothers were younger than me an' still wee bairns, my cousins only thought about the nice dresses displayed in the windows of the Market Street shops.

"One day I surprised her drawin' a strange symbol on the ceilin'. Like an eye or a flower drawn with a black marker. I learned later that it was called a Triquetra. It's still there, ye can see it. I asked her what it was fur.

'It protects ye from evil spirits, mochree. Dinnae worry, I'll do everythin' I can to protect ye, especially ye.'

'But protect me from what, Maw?'

"She didnae answer. The very same day she tied a red ribbon on the doors to distance the evil spirits, an' put a pair of socks under the beds against any evil spirits that could attach themselves to us while we slept.

"I noticed that those livin' in the village had changed: when we crossed them, they looked away from us, at the market, no one talked to us anymore, an' once a lady even shoved my mither away.

'Go back home Margaret, we dinnae want any of yer black magic here.'

"I asked my mither what black magic was. She told me not to listen to those people. She often spent time in the room overlookin' the lake, that was our room, fur the lads an' me. She spent hours lookin' out the window, lost in her thoughts. She looked at the dark water.

"After that, ye know what happened. One night when we were all asleep, my mither locked all the doors an' went outwith. I was fifteen. She left me a letter I know by heart now, fur havin' read it until my eyes were red.

"I'm dying because I bother
Those around me
Those people without parsimony
Do the same to me!
I hate the wind and the rain;
I hate the heat and the cold;
I therefore abandon my life
Without regrets and without fear. Please forgive me."

"When I read these words, I wanted to rush out to prevent her from doin' somethin' stupid, but no matter how hard I tried, I couldnae open the door. The wee lads started to cry. I went to the window an' saw her, floatin' on the loch's surface, like a water lily. It was too late; she was gone forever.

"I fell to the floor sobbin', then hugged my brothers, strokin' their foreheads. Our door then miraculously opened, as if my mither's death had released somethin'.

"At the age of fifteen, I was the new head of the family. I got my brothers hired as apprentices, one at the butcher's, the other at the blacksmith's. My cousins found jobs as maids while I was hired at St Leonard's Laundry.

"A few weeks after my mither's death, gossip an' story tellin' started up again in the village, this time against me. At the beginnin', I didnae understand why. Why were these people so mean? I had made a friend at the laundry an' talked to her about this. I insisted so much that I wanted to understand why the villagers had such a grudge against my family that she finally broke down an' told me. They accused my family of bein' responsible fur all sorts of bad things that had happened in the village, because the loch was on our land an' it was harmful. My mither an' aunt were said to have concluded a pact with the devil an' the creatures livin' in the loch to obtain what they wanted an' live near this place. I defended myself—that was ridiculous!

"I still lived in the house, where else could I have gone? After these revelations, I thought back on the strange reactions my mither had had, on her fascination fur the loch. But I still didnae believe any of this gossip. One evenin', I heard some voices an' saw some shadows. An' fur the next sixty years it never stopped. I understood that I was now experiencin' what my mither had endured, now that she wasnae there anymore. Now I was the one havin' these visions. Each day the feelin' of presences in the house got stronger, an' I couldnae do a thing about it. At the same time, I began to investigate the history of the house, discreetly askin' questions to people I knew. I didnae learn much that could have helped me, except that some lassies who had done witchcraft used to live here.

"One day I understood what must have made my mither snap: I saw my faither amongst those shadows. I visualized my mither—this strong woman who had endured bein' harassed by all the ghosts that inhabited the house, who had drawn signs to protect herself an' us—an' understood that she had given up when her dead husband came to haunt her.

"Life, though difficult, went on. I tried to understand an' control the situation. I did everything possible to enjoy the good times, to make the people in the village forget who I was, to be like everyone else, I went to the golf tournaments or to swimmin' competitions in the sea, even if people still turned around to look at me. I never married an' it wasnae easy. On Sundays often my brothers an' their wives, my cousins an' friends, came over.

"After a few years, my cousin Abigail told me about the

239

existence of a notebook. She'd inherited this notebook from her mither, Emily, an' had kept it locked away in a little trunk fur all these years. Seein' this trunk made me think about my mither, as she'd put some of her things in it too. This notebook traced the curse on the women in our family, with portraits of those who had died. There was also a large sheet of paper, rolled up like a piece of parchment, with the notebook an' it told the sad story of the Lewis family, Harriet, Robert, an' their bairns. I knew that Abigail didnae believe any of this, she didnae present any 'symptoms.' But I did an knew that I was endangered. The curse rolled itself out slowly, attackin' one target at a time. I had to be strong an' resist.

"So as not to perpetuate it, I had to resign myself to not havin' any bairn. That seemed the only possibility so that the curse would disappear. I kept my word fur many long years. But when love knocks at yer door, ye open it, dinnae ye? Time had gone by; I'd learned to live with the shadows. When I was forty, I met a bonnie laddie, a nice, delicate, considerate one, who knew what he wanted in life. John... He was the only lad that I'd ever loved, the only one I could talk to without fear, an' the only one who wasnae afraid of me, who didnae believe in all the gossip. But I was so much older than he was... He had just turned nineteen, a teen, whereas I was an adult. Fate decided fur us: he was a pilot at Leuchars air base, an' when war was declared, he had to leave. This same fate though, left me a daughter. Before she was born, I wondered if I would be transmittin' this curse to her. But when she arrived, all I could think about was protectin' her.

"I raised my daughter alone; John never knew about her. Up until now, I succeeded in protectin' her an' myself from this curse. It wasnae an easy task; it required a lot of mental strength an' respect fur the shadows. I was finally able to understand what they wanted, what I could do fur them an' what I couldnae, an' above all, I understood what the enigmatic quote in the notebook meant.

'It is said that all descendants of these women will become insane or die after dawn.'

"That's what saved my daughter an' I until now. I'm no longer tormented, but the evil spirit has now targeted other weaker members of the family: Lauren, one of Amber's granddaughters, an' today, Rebecca. I cannae help them anymore because I no longer react to the shadows in the loch, I dinnae feel them nor do I see them now. But I can help ye save her, as ye see them."

— CHAPTER SIXTEEN —

I listened attentively to her story, without interrupting her, and it was like the proverbial light bulb had gone on in my head, as each detail of her tale added a cornerstone to the final and logical edifice. Elizabeth sat down in the armchair next to the window.

"Did you know that Alex insinuates that you're senile? He also says you're in a wheelchair."

"That doesnae surprise me, lassie. I think he was a bit jealous that I gave him somethin' fur ye."

"You gave him something for me? I never got it!"

"I know, that's why I'm here. Of course I love my grandson, but I've always paid more attention to his sister, as because he's a boy, nothin' will happen to him. Here's what I asked him to give ye."

It was a cage with a little white butterfly with orange-tipped wings in it, who was flitting around frantically.

"This butterfly is the key. It'll allow ye to save Rebecca. It's a male Aurora, an Anthocharis cardamines. The orange spots on its wings remind people of dawn, which is how it got its name. The Orange Tip butterflies usually come out of their chrysalides in May, but Rebecca cannae wait till then, so I made sure I got some eggs a little earlier. Before becomin' a butterfly, Auroras eat Lady's Smock plants. That's a plant that has been used fur centuries in salads or as a medical herb. Lady's Smock plants grow all around the loch, an' in the olden days, witches came here to pick them. With it, they could cure scurvy, bronchitis, skin diseases, or even hysteria or epilepsy. A very special butterfly, as ye can see. All ye have to do is release it just before sunrise, right when the shadows are goin' back into the loch. At this precise moment, it's possible to break the evil charms an' save Rebecca."

"But... You mean that Rebecca's not a witch?"

"What, a witch? Of course nae."

"She put all sorts of protections in Mathieu's room, a knife under his pillow, and I've often seen her go down to the lake."

"Rebecca is cursed. She sees all the shadows of the dead who haunt her, lurin' her towards the loch. They want her to join them, become one of them. She didnae directly lead ye to the loch, the ghosts made her do it. An' these ghosts also gave ye suicidal thoughts when ye were in the tub. They wanted to regenerate ye with water, bring ye with them, because ye discovered their secret."

So, there was hope for Rebecca. If Elizabeth had outsmarted the curse for such a long time, I had to trust her. By saving

Rebecca, in a certain way, I'd be saving myself too. Then I could go back with the peace of mind of someone who had accomplished something important.

"Elizabeth, when you recognized your parents in the shadows, didn't you wish to join them?"

"Dinnae think about stuff like that, Anne. Ye cannae change the past. An' youthfulness is a gift ye dinnae want to sacrifice. I must admit it was hard fur me when I saw them, I was both sad an' happy at the same time. I missed them so much an' I was so alone! But I resisted, an' I had my daughter, I couldnae abandon her. Just thinkin' of her helped me overcome the temptation. What we've lost also makes us what we now are."

I nodded. She got up and put her hands in mine.

"Anne, I've told ye everythin'. I'm so glad to have met ye. It's up to ye now. Be careful: releasin' this butterfly isnae an easy task. The shadows will try to pull ye into their world. The forest surroundin' the loch front is yer unconscious mind an' yer own fears could trick ye. Stay strong, ye can do it. Ye're the only one who can save Rebecca."

"Thank you for your help."

She slowly walked to the door, her head bowed by her age that little by little seemed to reappear.

"Elizabeth, I met John, John Forrest. The ghosts come from his place, from the well outside. He loved you... He remembers the dress with the purple flowers that you used to wear. You should go see him, he's not in good health."

She smiled.

"Thanks fur the advice."

Then she left. I sat down on the bed, looking at the Orange Tip butterfly in its cage. The movement of its beautiful wings soothed me. This butterfly was like a human soul freed from its body, full of wisdom. I suddenly realized I hadn't even offered to accompany the old lady back home! I ran down the stairs into the street: no one.

The sun was shining brightly. Its light was so strong that it stunned me, nearly making me dizzy. I had to close my eyes and put my hand on my forehead to protect myself. Despite the sun, I was freezing in this cold December weather, and went in. Not a sound in the house. I was hungry. While making myself some bacon and eggs, I thought about what Elizabeth had revealed to me. I was so impressed that I had forgotten tons of things I wanted to ask her, for example about when I'd locked Mathieu's door and the whole house had started to vibrate... My diagram of the martyrs... My insomnia—was she insomniac too?

I sat on the couch with my plate. I could see Pete and Rebecca's house from the window. Tonight I would save a family. Pete would be so relieved if I could tell him I'd be helping his sister. They'd spent Christmas together, without a worry in the world. Well, without their mother, but... I couldn't bring her back, though, unfortunately. Like Elizabeth had explained, you can't change the past.

I'd be flying back tomorrow. Tomorrow. Hard for me to realize that. I'd see Guillaume, my parents, my old friends. They all seemed so far away now. But I was eager to go back home, to be with all these people once again, to tell them about my adventures. I'd already packed my bags.

I went into town, one last time. The cold wind was whipping through the hibernating landscape, nude and thin trees, and the frozen grass and its icy glitter. I luckily had my red beret that I could pull down to cover my ears, as well as my red gloves. I walked up through Kennedy Gardens, still enchanted by this peaceful lush garden. At Doubledykes Road, I turned left towards the golf course, then went up to West Sands.

I wanted to admire this place one last time, fondly remembering the first day I'd been there: I'd fallen asleep on the beach and a storm woke me up! I'd come a long way. When I arrived, I was lost, at loose ends, alone. I now had a goal and felt serene and peaceful. I'd met good people. Some made me sad, it's true. But my long journey was winding up, marking the beginning of a new life without the weight of my former one. The sea was still fighting against the rocks from the cliff and the tongue of sand, the one that the movie *Chariots of Fire* had been shot on—though I'd never seen it. And all this fresh air, pulsing through my body and mind! Then I turned to take The Scores street, on St Andrews Bay.

A few golfers were playing on the Old Course, dressed to the nines, wearing clothes that must have cost just as much as their equipment. I made my way up to the Martyr's Monument and read again the inscription honoring Hamilton, Forrest, Wishart and Myln, the men I had been thinking about for so many months. I hope they'd rest in peace, that they'd crossed the lake.

I wanted to soak up every detail in the road: the alley of trees, gray stone facades of the houses, passersby, the cars. I went up to the ruins of the castle, admiring them for a moment, then walked around the GW slab and got to the north end of the cathedral. I thought about the White Lady who wandered there and Robert de Montrose in his tower. I also remembered those tourists who asked me to take their picture—how I hated meeting French people at that time! I strolled along the wall to reach the Pier, then the port. I imagined Elizabeth and her brothers here waiting for their father's ship to make it back, him pulling up his nets, unloading his catch for the day. At the moment there were only a few small boats still in service, bobbing up and down and bumping into each other in the light waves. The same ice-cream guy was still there, summer or winter. Whoever ate ice cream when it was freezing?

I went back to Market Street. I was still amazed by the contrast: this road full of people, noise, smells and light, whereas its perpendicular or parallel sisters were much calmer. It would soon be Christmas. The shops and houses were decorated, fake Santa Clauses hung from windows, and we could hear *Jingle Bells* or *I Wish You a Merry Christmas* through loudspeakers in the street. People smiled blissfully, their arms carrying packages, or just window shopping. In a nutshell, Christmas. Everyone was happy at Christmas time. Not me. Every Christmas was hard on me: it was hard to see my family and friends all happy, and not being a part of their excitement and joy. The magic of

Christmas never worked for me and left me even more despondent since I'd lost my daughter.

I turned onto South Street and bumped into Pete.

"Hey, Pete!"

"Oh, hi Anne. How you doing?"

"Fine, what about you? Did you just get up?"

He was wearing a brown bathrobe and a nightcap, right in the middle of town! People turned around to look at him.

"Nae, just too lazy to get dressed. Cool outfit, isn't it? Look, everyone likes it."

"Pete, I found out how I can help Rebecca. Tomorrow all this will just be a bad memory."

"All this... Hmm."

"Is she at home? I'd like to see her, talk to her."

"I don't know where she is."

"I met Elizabeth! She explained everything."

"Well, good. Listen, I'm sort of in a hurry here. I've got an appointment at the tattoo artist for a piercing in my eyebrow."

He was acting strange. Not even listening to me. Distracted, looking right and left, impatient. So different from the Pete who let me in his house. I took a hold of his arm and looked him straight in the eyes.

"Pete, that's good news, isn't it? You're not happy?"

He pulled away.

"Whatever."

"What do you mean *whatever*? Did something happen to Rebecca? It's too late?"

I suddenly imagined the worst. But he answered with contempt.

"What the hell are you talking about? Leave me alone, I have to go. See ya."

"Pete, come on! You're the one who wanted me to help Rebecca escape from the curse."

"The curse? What's the matter with you? Alex was right when he told me yesterday that you'd gone nuts."

And with this, he turned around, leaving me dumbfounded. How could he have changed so much?

It was like a blow to my stomach; I was suddenly exhausted. I decided to go back to Lochan Wynd to rest. After all, I'd be up all night to make sure I was in the right place when the sun rose. For Rebecca, I couldn't fail. I was her only hope.

The house was empty, once again. I sometimes wondered if I actually had flatmates or if I'd invented them: they were never there anymore. That didn't bother me though. I had a one-to-one with the living house. I could feel her breathe and move around me, and I was protected like a fetus in its mother's womb. I knew the house well now, and it knew me.

My old friend, my migraine, was back again, and I lay down

on the couch in the living room. I just needed to sleep a little, to rest and repair my body with it. I felt better as soon as I'd closed my eyes. But a bit later, I was assaulted by nightmares, again.

I fell down an endless hole.

— CHAPTER SEVENTEEN —

Lochan Wynd was plunged into darkness. I had something important to do the forthcoming night, and with Elizabeth's recommendations, I serenely prepared myself, like a soldier before waging battle. I had to concentrate, the future of a whole family depended on it, without forgetting myself, by extension.

If I failed, would I be taking the plane back to France at noon, as planned? I didn't know. Was I going to forget Rebecca, Elizabeth, Mathieu and Pete and just leave, as if their lives had never been between my hands? Let them fend for themselves? Would I have a clear conscience, or would I spend my whole life wondering what had happened to them?

There was only one outcome to this long night: I couldn't fail.

I walked upstairs to get the Orange Tip butterfly, the one I'd need for the upcoming events. He was still there in his cage, fluttering around impatiently.

"Just wait a couple of hours, you'll soon be free."

I looked at myself in the mirror and hardly recognized the lady across from me. I'd lost so much weight! It was true I'd hardly eaten anything for the past few days, but I wasn't hungry. My eyes had deep purple rings under them, stigmas of my many nights of insomnia. I looked terrible, but what did I expect, being a night owl? I turned away from the mirror to cast a glance at the lake, outside. *Eyes, look your last! Arms, take your last embrace!*[3] This dark lake, darker than the sky, the one I had to face that night. I watched it for a while, until I was ready.

I stepped out. If a sunbeam wounded me, I would succumb on the moss[4]. It was peculiar: all those quotes from books I'd read popped up in my brain, as if what I was going through corresponded to what others had written. I let my eyes get used to the dark, then started walking down the path to the lake. Had I forgotten the Aurora butterfly? I checked: the cage with the white butterfly with orange wings was in my right hand.

I carefully walked in the thick silence that seemed to be resisting me, as if I had to make my way through wads of cotton. The grass that I stepped on crackled lightly each time I put my foot down and little stones rolled away, as if fleeing my approach.

I finally reached the woods in front of the lake. So peaceful! The night was calm. The trees surrounded me with their

---

[3] Shakespeare, *Romeo and Juliette*, Act V, scene 3. What Romeo said to his Juliette, believing she was dead, before joining her by drinking poison.

[4] Arthur Rimbaud, *Bannières de Mai. In the original text: "Si un rayon de lune me blessait, je succomberais sur la mousse"*

protection and the whirring of their leaves composed a soothing melody, up there towards the moon. I put the butterfly cage down and sat on a tree trunk that had fallen. Then all I could do was wait.

I was enchanted by this little forest that seemed so alive. I felt good there, nearly joyful, fulfilled by so much beauty and by this mesmerizing simplicity. The moon played with the breeze, making the shadows flit around. Life was omnipresent, in this tiny insect climbing up my leg, in the moss on the northern sides of the trees, in the earthy and moist smell of the night. Was this Heaven? Soothed, bewitched, minutes then hours went by.

Then things began to slowly change. Each tree suddenly was strangely present. The woods were no longer a group of trees, but an endless quantity of singular and unique beings.

It was starting.

The moon quit playing with the wind. The crackling of the leaves became a murmur, and the trees began to move. Where was the Aurora butterfly? I picked up the little cage and looked inside: it was still there.

The murmurs slowly became voices, and trees became bodies. I was familiar with these shadows already: I'd followed them, I'd touched them, I knew why they were there. They were my friends now.

"Are you sure of that?"

Yes, I was, I'd learned to understand them, and they were

grateful. All the dead from St Andrews were now beginning to move, so when the time was right, they'd be able to go into the lake. There were people with burned faces, mothers with their children, men who limped, people who'd drowned and were still dripping water, couples holding hands.

I saw them, but they ignored me, moving around me in an incoherent agitation. I now had to prepare myself too and concentrate, to be ready at the right time, I couldn't fail. Was the butterfly still there? I checked once again, mechanically looking into the cage: affirmative.

"You don't know a thing about us, nothing."

They were all now looking at me. Of course they were, I knew... I knew that...

"You don't understand our pain. Our impatience after so many years of waiting."

The shadows were pushing and jostling me. I wasn't welcome here. Elizabeth had warned me that it wouldn't be an easy task. The darkness was beginning to scare me.

"We know why you are here."

The butterfly! I compulsively checked once again, then squeezed the handle of the cage in the palm of my hand. I had to appease the shadows so they'd leave me alone.

"Who are you really?"

But I'm... I'm Anne... The shadows came closer, staring me in the eyes. My apprehension increased. Who was I really? Hard to answer this easy question. It was ridiculous...

"You don't exist. This doesn't exist. Whatever you think you know, you're mistaken."

Those penetrating eyes... I was suddenly boiling over, I could feel my heart pounding in my ears and thought I was going to faint. Dizzy, I fell and sat down. Out of breath, my mouth dry, I tried to collect my wits. I shouldn't listen to these voices. I should do what I'd come for, put an end to the curse and liberate Rebecca. I was doing this in honor of Elizabeth. I had the key, it was easy, all I had to do was let the Aurora butterfly out at the break of dawn, above the lake.

"You're not from here."

Stop talking to me. Pretend I'm not here. I don't want to disturb you, I just want to help someone.

"You shouldn't be here."

I felt like crying. Was the butterfly still there? Had I left it at home, all of this would be for nothing then! Where was it? I couldn't see it! I suddenly realized I was holding the cage, which calmed me down a bit. I put my arms around it, gripping it to my chest, crouching on the ground. I was shaking, so consumed by anxiety I was paralyzed. I felt more confused than ever.

"You disappointed us. Do you know why?"

No, I don't want to know. Shut up! I'm here for Rebecca... I put my hands over my ears so I wouldn't hear those sharp voices hurting me like daggers.

"Go away. You're not at home here. You disappointed us because you're a bad mother."

They kept on talking, were the voices coming from inside my head? *A bad mother?* Some of the shadows turned away from me with contempt. Others came nearer.

"She's a bad mother. We know it. Leave her alone."

But I never had a child... Had I had one? I couldn't remember, I couldn't trust my memories. I had no idea who I was anymore.

"See, you're wrong. You forgot that you had a baby."

Lara ... my darling daughter ... how could I have forgotten her? I broke out in bitter and uncontrollable sobs. That didn't stop the voices, though, they continued torturing me.

"You abandoned her."

How could I have known she wouldn't make it? I loved her, I wanted her.

"You can still help your child, think about her, listen to her. You should have saved her."

Shut up, just shut up! I lowered my head, closed my eyes and started hitting my ears with my hands so I wouldn't hear them anymore. I would have liked to shrivel away. I was ashamed, I cried, I cried until I'd emptied all the liquid from my body. *My daughter is dead... My baby...* These thoughts kept coming back, overwhelming me. I didn't know what to do anymore. What was I doing here? I had no idea. I was so very alone. Life had no meaning. And it was so terribly long when you were unhappy. Why keep on living? *To be or not to be, that was the question...*

"You're not alone. She's waiting for you."

She's waiting for me? I opened my eyes. The beautiful lake was right in front of me. The woods had disappeared, as had the shadows. The voices were silent. I slowly got back up. The butterfly's cage dropped to the ground without me noticing it. It was cold and damp. I was afraid of the dark.

I carefully walked to the lake, this huge dark mass whose surface seemed so smooth.

I suddenly saw her. She was there, a five-year-old girl sitting cross-legged in the middle of the lake, playing like kids her age do, laughing and talking to herself. When she saw me, she stopped playing and got up. Behind her the sun rose and its first beams slowly warmed me up. Day was breaking. Lara ran to me with open arms. She forgave me.

The light was so very reassuring, filling me with happiness, love and serenity. Everything was so beautiful! I could see life itself flowing like a river inside of each and every thing. The lake was the source of creation.

I ran to her too. *Arms, take your last embrace!*

I held Lara in my arms, as tight as possible. I could smell her pure scent of a child. Holding her was the most beautiful thing in the entire world. We were finally together.

— CHAPTER EIGHTEEN —

"Hello, Guillaume."

"Hello, Doctor."

"Guillaume, I'm speaking to you as a friend. You've been coming here every day for a year now, ever since Anne was committed. I have to be honest with you. Anne seems to be escaping from us, going further and further each time. I don't think it's a good idea for you to see her in this lethargic state. In spite of our care, her psychoses seem to be getting worse. You must have realized this yourself: at the beginning of her therapy, she recognized you, got out of bed. Now we're finding it harder and harder to pull her out of her hallucinations. She seems to want to live in her dreams and abandon all contact with reality. I'm so terribly sorry."

"Did you try anything stronger? She's been lying in this bed, locked in this room, hallucinating for so long. Isn't there some way for you to wake her up? Pull her out of her mental delusions?"

"I have to admit that we've never had a case as serious as this for postnatal psychosis. She's hovering between paranoia and schizophrenia. She seems to be hearing voices, her hallucinations can last for days or even months, like this one did. This time she pronounced names that we've never heard before: Mathieu, Rebecca, Elizabeth... You said that you'd never heard of them."

"No, we don't know anyone with these names. Same thing for 'Hamilton' or 'Lochan Wynd' or all of these words she keeps repeating during her never-ending nightmares. I have no idea where she could have imagined all these elements she seems so attached to. Before all of this happened, we'd talked about going to Scotland for a couple of days, but never got around to it. It's weird that in her delusions she chose a country she's never visited. Without getting out of bed, she invents all these stories. Are you sure that it's not dangerous for her? She's agitated, her body is always covered with sweat and the nurses have to change her sheets twice a day. If only she were having sweet dreams..."

"You know with a trauma like losing a child it's only normal that she's having a hard time. But for Anne, her greatest danger is her own imagination. She's the only one who can control her thoughts. We're going to keep on doing our best so she'll get better, I guarantee you. I'd like Professor Pavin in Paris to take over. He's France's number one specialist for serious psychoses. But she'll have to be transferred to the capital for that. If you agree of course. You're the decision maker here Guillaume, and I know it's not going to be easy. Once she's in Paris, you won't be able to see her as often."

"I've been here for months, but that hasn't helped her at all.

I just want her to get better, that's all. I can make concessions, let her see the best specialist in Paris if that's what she needs."

"Thanks for trusting me. You'll let her parents know? I'll leave you two while I get the paperwork done. Good luck."

"Thank you, Doctor."

Guillaume sat down next to Anne. He'd never be able to get used to seeing her like this, a mere room number. What could be going on inside her little head? Her hair had grown so much since she'd been here. He delicately put a stray strand of hair behind her ear.

Last night was the worst of all. Then suddenly, when the sun came up, Anne had calmed down. Since then, she had a slight Mona Lisa like smile on her lips, an inaccessible and unfathomable one, as if she had a secret that Guillaume would have like to have shared with her.

He picked up her hand. It was freezing.

— CHAPTER NINETEEN —

A couple—a girl who looked like one of Botticelli's painting and a puny French guy—were walking hand-in-hand in a romantic setting, one that echoed the love they had for each other.

They weren't in a hurry, living for the present, flowers in their hair.

And I, I was floating on the lake like a white lily that had flowered too soon...

— GLOSSARY
OF SCOTTISH WORDS —

- ❖ **Loch:** Lake
- ❖ **Aye:** Yes
- ❖ **Nae:** No
- ❖ **Lad, Laddie:** Young man
- ❖ **Lass, Lassie:** Young woman
- ❖ **Bonnie:** Beautiful
- ❖ **Bairn:** Child
- ❖ **Wee:** Small
- ❖ **Mochree:** My dear

— ACKNOWLEDGMENTS —

I would like to thank Jacquie Bridonneau who has made possible the translation of this novel in English.

I thank Judy in America, Linda and her friends in the UK for their valuable proofreading.

I thank Céline Fuentès and my fellow authors friends from Club des Indés for their advice about self-publishing.

I remain indebted to all these people for their help and their kindness.

Thanks as always to my husband for his support.

— AFTERWORD —

First of all, thank you for reading my book! I hope you enjoyed it.

Without readers, authors are nothing. Did you appreciate this story? If you have a moment, please leave a review on the online bookstores or book communities. And tell your friends and family why you enjoyed reading it. You can make a big difference. Honest reviews of my book help bring them to the attention of other readers.

As I mentioned at the beginning of this novel, the subject of perinatal bereavement is very important to me. At the beginning of 2011, when I began writing this book, I thought about my sister who had just lost an embryo because of an ectopic pregnancy.

On January 2nd, 2014, my son was stillborn. My entire pregnancy had gone well, and nothing prepared us for that. Despite an emergency C-section and everything that the nurses and doctors did, my baby, in acute respiratory distress, didn't survive. Even now, no one knows what happened.

While I was in the hospital, as I couldn't sleep, I thought about that strange parallel, the strange coincidence between what I had endured and Anne's story. I had finished about half of the book. Time went by, I reread my notes and wondered if I should change my plot. In my book, Anne lost her baby soon after birth. What would my family think? I didn't want to shock them. They'd think that I had written this book to tell others about what had happened to me, whereas when I'd started, it was something completely different, relating an event that was tragic enough to cause Anne to lose her mind.

I talked to my mom about this. She suggested changing the storyline, transforming Anne's "problem" into a serious disease, like cancer. I immediately thought of breast cancer. It was a good idea, but I couldn't get into it.

I thought things over and decided to keep my original storyline. Firstly, because I couldn't think of any other event that would trigger such a reaction, and then because writing about the death of a child would allow me to free myself, evict my pain and exorcise what had happened. I have to admit that I wanted to talk about this, write about it, give with my words an existence to my baby who died, making him immortal. So in 2014 I began to write again in this book.

When I read again my finished work, I didn't change many words. Strangely, what I had written before matched my feelings as an orphaned mother.

A year and a half later, in May 2015, I finished writing this book and published it independently. I was pregnant once again, a girl this time. We were both overjoyed and worried. Then for the fifth-month sonogram, the verdict was announced: my baby was suffering from a complex cardiopathy. I consulted many doctors and specialists and each time their analysis was honed a bit more: pulmonary atresia, atrio-ventricular failure, situs inversus... All of this inoperable and my baby wouldn't survive. I remained for two more weeks with this baby inside me, knowing that she'd be stillborn, singing songs to her. People who saw me in the street kindly asked me when I was due, whether it would be a boy or a girl. They didn't know and it was too hard for me to tell them. On June 25, 2015, my stillborn daughter was born naturally. After that I wrote *La Femme sans Visage*, [The Woman without a Face] a philosophical fable that did me good.

Time went by and then in 2016 I was expecting again, a boy this time. The doctors tried to reassure us, saying that there was no reason that this baby wouldn't make it. My husband refused to come with me to my medical appointments. I tried to reassure him, and he finally gave in and went with me to the second sonogram. I had a lump in my throat, my hands were damp and I stared at the wall. Everything fell apart when the doctor sighed. "I don't like the way this heart looks." He detected a leaking mitral valve with an aortic narrowing and sent us to one of his colleagues. He confirmed the diagnostic, the baby was suffering from a valvular aortic narrowing. Blood wasn't flowing well, exhausting the left ventricle. His heart would probably stop before he was born. On November 16, 2016, after six months, this baby was also stillborn.

We decided to adopt in 2017. The beginning of another saga, a long journey, but one that we took without hesitating, to give a child our love and make him or her happy.

And then in September 2019, the Regional Council called us for an appointment. We had been chosen as parents for a four-month-old baby. We met our daughter, Lucie, on September 30, 2019, and since then, she's lit up our lives and we couldn't be happier.

Coming back to the book that you've just finished, I'm sure you'll understand how important it is for me. Through the book, all the little angels who left too early still exist.

Scotland is a beautiful country; one I can only recommend for tourists.

Should you go to St Andrews (a magnificent little town, not too far from Edinburgh) and try to find Lochan Wynd, you won't, for the good reason that it doesn't exist. To invent it, though, I used Melville Hall in St Andrews, which was where I lived as a student. If you go there, right across from Melville Hall, you'll see a little pond, one that I often admired from my window.

As for the title, at first I thought of "A French Girl in Scotland," or "Scottish Time." I wanted this story to be a lesson about life and happiness. But then I decided to make this a deeper and supernatural story and thought about "The Mystery of Lochan Wynd," a mystery of the human soul and secret rituals. I wanted to warn readers that there wouldn't be a happy end to the story. But I was afraid that Lochan Wynd wouldn't mean anything to anyone. So I chose "The Lake Still Sobs."

I've always liked stories about witches, vampires, and ghosts so I sprinkled the novel with "symbols."

When Anne picked a four-leaf clover, she opened her mind to an imaginary world.

"Oidhche Shamhna," that you heard on Halloween is Scottish Gaelic for the night before Samain, celebrated on October 31st, when winter begins. On this night, the barrier between real life and supernatural life disappears, souls of the deceased come back to places where they used to live. Most people just call this Halloween.

In Mathieu's room, honey, milk, the scale and bells are elements linked to the supernatural. When you ring the bell, you communicate between the earth and the heavens. Scales symbolize duality. Milk is the beverage for immortality, and honey is food for the wise.

And finally, this story pays tribute to all those who have left this world, as well as those still remaining, without them.

I'm so glad we took this trip together!

— ABOUT MARIE HAVARD —

Marie Havard was born in Béziers, in the south of France, in 1983. She studied Literature at St Andrews University (Scotland) and at Perpignan University (France).

The Lake Still Sobs is the first of her books to be published in English.

She lives near Montpellier with her family.

Want to stay updated with Marie Havard?

Visit her website ***www.mariehavard.com***

or her Amazon Author Page:

www.amazon.com/Marie-Havard/e/B01DKX4ELE

Like her on *Facebook:* mariehavard.auteur

Follow her on *Twitter:* mariehavard_ and on *Instagram:* marie.havard

Made in the USA
Monee, IL
27 August 2022